Falling for her Fiancé

Falling for her Fiancé

CINDI MADSEN

Entangled Publishing, LLC
2614 South Timberline Road
Suite 105, PMB 159
Fort Collins, CO 80525
rights@entangledpublishing.com

Bliss is an imprint of Entangled Publishing, LLC.

Edited by Stacy Abrams
Cover design by Bree Archer
Cover photography by eclipse_images/iStock

Manufactured in the United States of America

First Edition January 2013

Bliss
an Entangled imprint

To everyone out there taking a chance on love.

Chapter One

Apparently, even spammers were bound and determined to shove her lack of a love life in her face today. Dating sites filled her junk folder. She could *View Beautiful Singles* or *WINK at singles now—free for three whole days!* Did winking usually cost more? Dating a millionaire would probably be nice, but the *Be one of our cougars!* from CougarDating.com stung. Hello? She wasn't *that* old.

There was also an exclamation-marked e-mail about increasing the size of something she didn't have. But apparently, it was a *very* pressing matter.

Dani clicked the box to select them all, hit the delete button, and watched them disappear. If only she could do the same to her work inbox. There were approximately thirty e-mails about the upcoming retreat now that more details had been announced, most of them in screaming caps and containing multiple exclamation points, because one just didn't convey enough freakin' excitement.

Of course they're excited. They all get to take their significant others and get in good with the boss.

While the company would never call the retreat couples exclusive, the one they'd had two years ago proved that being part of a duo meant more one-on-one time with the boss and his wife. Wayne Bridges always bragged about how Bridges Marketing, Inc. was a family-friendly business—he also had this whole competition-makes-you-stronger stance—and she knew one very pompous jerk had been promoted over her as a result, even if Wayne would deny it.

And maybe Mr. Pompous's marketing degree had edged him in, too, but Dani had done most of the work for every account they'd taken on together. All the work and none of the credit. But with a new senior exec position opening up, she was going to change that, no matter what it took. Because medical bills were expensive, and unless she won the lottery soon, the only way to get extra money was to move up, preferably ASAP. Mama was now living in Florida with Abuela Morales, taking over the physical care as well as working long hours to try to pay for everything. Dani was helping financially as much as she could, and between the two of them, they were still barely squeaking by every month. Mama told her not to stress, that it wasn't her responsibility, yet she felt the constant burden weighing her down. When she'd gotten all the scholarships she could for college—both for academics and basketball—and still came up short, her family had pooled their money so she could go. Abuela Morales, her maternal grandmother, was the one who'd given her the most.

Dani drummed her fingers on the desk, trying to figure out how she would push past the fact that she couldn't participate in most of the physical competitions at the retreat without a partner and still get the promotion anyway. Not to mention the fact that she tended to freeze up around her boss, like his presence cut off the part of her brain where full sentences were stored.

Her cell phone rang, Justin Timberlake's "SexyBack" filling the air. That song meant her day was about to get better, and it even had her cracking a smile when she answered.

"Tell me I don't have to go," Wes said. He was the one who'd programmed JT's song as his assigned ringtone the last time they were together, claiming the tune was "so me."

"You don't have to go," Dani said.

"Thanks. And thanks for not asking what you're giving me permission to miss."

Dani stood and leaned against the wall of her gray cubicle. From this viewpoint, she could see the setting sun through the window of the office she hoped to soon make hers. "You're talking about your sister's wedding. And like I said, you don't *have* to go, but you should, and we both know you're going to."

Wes's sigh came over the line. "If you ask me, she let me off the hook when she picked my ex-fiancée as her bridesmaid. Today when I was home, Audrey and my mom both gave me these pity-filled looks every time they mentioned her name. Like I'm not over her. And I *am*."

"Of course you're over that self-centered princess." Okay, so her description might be a little harsh, but she knew Wes needed to be reminded why he *should* be over his ex, Sophie, even though Dani wasn't sure he actually was. In fact, she sometimes worried he never would be, and that was a shame, because she'd never been good enough for him in the first place. The girl was way too high maintenance for Wes, all demand with no compromise.

"Enough about all that boring crap. How's life on your end?" he asked.

Dani told him about the retreat and how she felt all this pressure to stand out but didn't know how she was going to compete in boat races when everyone else had a partner. "Not to mention all the sad looks I'll get—a few of my coworkers' wives always want to set me up, too. A couple of months ago I told everyone I was dating someone just to get them off my back. If only I had an actual guy to go with me." She used her thumbnail to scrape away the remnants of her last manicure. "Guess you don't happen to be free at the end of this month."

She'd thrown it out as a joke, but the tingling of an idea was working its way through her head, and she started to wonder if it might be brilliant. She snuck back inside her cubical and lowered her voice, even though most everyone had already left for the day. "Wes, fly over here and go with me. I'll tell them... I'll tell them you're my fiancé or something. We'd rule all the physical competitions, I wouldn't be so nervous with you there, and I'll finally get Wayne's attention."

The other end of the line was dead silent. She glanced at the display to make sure they were still connected and then put the phone back to her ear. "I know it's kind of extreme, but I haven't seen you in forever and—"

"I'll be your fiancé for the retreat if you'll be mine for Audrey's wedding," Wes said. "I was going to try to find a date, but this would be so much better. It'll stop the pity-filled looks, and you know me well enough to pull it off—plus everyone's always suspected we were more than friends anyway. It's the perfect way to show Sophie I've moved on since she dumped me."

Dani bit her lip. "I'm not sure taking off work right before I go up for a promotion is—"

"You never take time off. Come on, Dani. I need you here."

She was also thinking about the cost for the flight to North Carolina, but Wes had said he needed her, so how could she skip it now? Not to mention, it'd been *way* too long since they'd seen each other—calls and texts just weren't enough with her best friend.

The more she thought about it, the more this seemed like the perfect solution for both of them. She could picture showing up at the wedding with Wes to see Sophie's lips twisting up in that tight-ass way they always did. She imagined sitting behind the desk in the office across from her cubical, giving instructions instead of doing all the grunt work. And even better, she pictured the extra zeros behind her paycheck every month and finally being able to help her family without barely scraping by.

"I'm getting down on one knee right now," Wes said, but she could also hear the crunch of chips, meaning he was most likely sitting on his couch, spilling crumbs all over himself. "Danielle I-forget-your-middle-name Vega—"

"You don't know my middle name?"

"You've got, like, three of them, and they're all in Spanish."

"I've only got two, and names are names."

"Oh, like you remember mine."

"Jonathan."

"Okay, fine, you win this round. Now if you'd stop busting my chops, I'm trying to ask you something here." The sound of more crunching chips came over the line. "So like I was saying…Danielle two-middle-names Vega, will you do me the honor of pretending you're going to marry me?"

She laughed, a lightness filling her chest. Of all the stunts they'd pulled, this one would take the cake. First the wedding cake, and then that awful bakery kind they passed around the office whenever one of her coworkers had a birthday or, you know, blinked right. Even though Wes couldn't see her, she went all out, throwing a hand to her chest, batting her eyes, and doing her best over-the-moon-with-a-side-of-ditzy voice. "Yes! Yes! A thousand times, yes!"

As the plane descended toward Charlotte, North Carolina, excitement danced through Dani's stomach. She leaned forward in her seat and peered out the tiny window. She'd grown up a few hours away in Greensboro and had gone to Wingate University, which was about forty minutes south. The green trees, all the historic sites, and the fact that Wes was here—it felt like coming home.

The flight attendant did the last check through the cabin and Dani started bouncing her leg—until her seatmate, a crabby older woman, glared. *She probably doesn't have a best friend, period, much less one she's dying to see.*

Or should I say fiancé? Dani shook her head. Being engaged to Wes was an odd thing to think about. When they'd met freshman year over their nerdy love of history, they'd become instant friends. They studied together, hung out most weekends, and occasionally crashed at each other's places if they were too tired or too tipsy to make it home.

People always assumed they were a couple. No one seemed to get that they simply loved each other without being *in* love, and that Wes was still the one friend who made everything better, who was by her side when she needed him most.

Finally the wheels touched down and they taxied toward the gate. Anticipation tingled through her veins, and it was all she could do to patiently wait for her turn to exit. Whatever happened with their fake engagement and his sister's wedding, this was going to be the vacation she so desperately needed. Already her body felt lighter, her head clearer.

As soon as she got off the plane, she zipped past the other people, weaving in and out, practically running now. She walked past security and scanned the faces. Nope. Nope. Nope.

"Dani!"

She turned toward the voice, her feet already propelling her forward. Wes met her halfway, scooping her up in a giant hug. She squeezed him so tightly the brim of her baseball cap ended up crooked. She took a step back to get a better look at him. His wavy, dirty-blond hair was longer than usual, and from the looks of it, he hadn't shaved in weeks. He grinned and his pale blue eyes lit up—good to know he was as excited to see her as she was to see him.

"I almost didn't recognize you with all the scruff. You look like you should have an ax over your shoulder and a big blue ox for a pet." She ran her hand down his face and his whiskers tickled her palm. "Do girls go for that these days?"

"Not many, unfortunately," he said, but she knew that wasn't true. Although Wes hadn't had a serious relationship since Sophie, there was never a shortage of girls after him.

He took her suitcase from her. "Audrey and my mom are both on me to shave and get a haircut before the wedding."

They started toward the exit and he eyed her get-up of T-shirt, yoga pants, and neon yellow sneakers. "If I'm Paul Bunyan, you must be Workout Barbie."

She elbowed him in the gut. "Hey, I was flying and bloated. Give me a break."

He flashed her a grin and draped his arm over her shoulders. "I'm so glad you're here. I figured we'd do a little hiking, and then I've got something special planned for tonight."

Something special usually meant something she'd end up regretting later. "Have you talked to your family yet? Do they even know I'm coming to the wedding?"

His grin widened. Wes loved to be the center of attention, loved a good prank, and this was a mixture of both. Of *course* he hadn't warned them. "They're going to flip. But we don't have to deal with anyone until tonight after dinner, so we'll worry about that later."

Over the phone this had seemed like the perfect solution, something that would be simple. But now that she was here, thinking of meeting Wes's entire family, a ball of nerves was forming in her gut. Since she wasn't actually going to marry him, it shouldn't matter whether his family liked her or not, should it?

She pressed down all her worries the best she could and shot him a smile. "Actually, I'm more worried that my fiancé looks like a hobo."

• • •

Over the past few weeks, all the stupid wedding stuff had been throwing Wes off, leaving him constantly on edge. Okay, so if he were being honest, it was mostly the Sophie thing. He still couldn't believe Audrey had made his ex a bridesmaid. Yes, the reason he'd met her was because she and Audrey were friends, but it felt like choosing sides, and since he was the one dumped on his ass without any more explanation than "It's just not going to work," Audrey should've chosen his. To add insult to injury, about a month after breaking off the engagement, Sophie had shown up at the bar he frequented with some dude hanging all over her.

But the instant he and Dani were hiking up the trail, none of that mattered anymore. Especially now that they were nearing the Buzzard Rock outcropping, where they could sit in the sun and get a view of the entire area.

Dani blew out a breath. "This is your idea of a small hike?"

"Anything not requiring rappelling gear is small."

She shook her head, but she was smiling. He knew she'd be down for however big or small he decided to go, which was why she was his favorite person to just hang out with. It was hard to explain their relationship to people—especially to his guy friends, who couldn't believe he'd never "hit that." It wasn't like he'd failed to notice that Dani was naturally pretty, her Mexican ethnicity giving her an exotic look he'd seen plenty of dudes drool over. A fact that Sophie had definitely noticed. They'd argued about his relationship with Dani all the time.

What people didn't get, though, was that being with her was effortless. They liked the same things, laughed at the same jokes—she just got him in a way no one else did. When something good or bad happened, she was the first person he wanted to call, and it had been like that pretty much since the day he'd met her.

At the top, he pulled out two water bottles and handed one to Dani. She took a swig and looked over the valley. Her shoulders relaxed and she closed her eyes, tipping her head to the sun. He knew she'd like this place as much as he did.

"I miss this," she said. "I should find trails in Arkansas, but it takes so long to get out of the city, I never have anyone to go with, and I just don't think it'll ever feel like home the way North Carolina does."

"So move back."

She looked at him, head tilted. "Oh sure, just leave my job and move back. Easy for you to say."

"What's keeping you? You moved out there because of Steve, and now that he's out of the picture, you might as well come back home." She turned away, so he couldn't see her expression. He knew the idiot she'd followed to Arkansas had hurt her, and he hoped she wasn't staying to try to get back together with him. Wes had felt the urge to punch the guy from day one, but he'd tried to get along with him for Dani's sake. If he ever saw Steve again, he was going to enjoy telling him exactly how much of a loser he was, though.

"My job's in Little Rock." She plopped down, and Wes

sat next to her. She picked up a handful of dirt and let it drift through her fingers. "How about you? Still glad you left your desk job to fly helicopters?"

"Hell yeah." When he'd first considered quitting his perfectly good software sales job to train for his pilot's license, his family had flipped. Dani was the only one who'd told him to go for it if that was what he wanted. She also said that if everyone else disowned him and he ended up broke, he'd always have a spot on her couch to sleep and her fridge to raid.

"I love my job," he said. "Love being up in the air, flying over the city in a matter of minutes. And now that I've got more piloting experience, I'm thinking of starting my own tour company. Something a little more exciting—all the places in North Carolina people don't normally see with historical facts made more interesting by yours truly." He grinned at her to drive the point home. "Maybe even places where people can cliff dive or go white water rafting—spots that are nearly impossible to get to any other way."

He'd been thinking about it for a while, but he'd kept it in, not wanting to hear how crazy or unrealistic the idea was. Buying a couple of helicopters and opening up your own company wasn't exactly cheap. Dani twisted the lid on her water bottle and nodded, one corner of her mouth turned up. "Sounds perfect for you."

His heart swelled, excitement leaping up to take the place of all his doubts. "Yeah?"

"I can totally see it." She tucked her leg up, twisting toward him. "Remember that first night we studied at your apartment instead of the library? When we planned out our futures? You told me you were going to be the next Indiana Jones—not an actor, but the real thing. Who played guitar in a famous band on the side. And after talking for hours without managing to actually get any of our assignment done,

I knew we were destined to be more than just study partners. Even though I was pretty sure you were half crazy."

"*I* was crazy? You said you wanted to teach history at a high school and coach basketball."

Her lips curved into a smile, nostalgia filling her features. "You promised you'd bring all the archeological items you dug up to my classroom so I'd be able to get a peek and share them with my students before the museums fought over them."

"I might've had a few too many beers that night." What he didn't confess was how nervous he'd been to have her at his place that first time, back when he was trying to impress her for other reasons.

She laughed. "Probably another reason we didn't get any work done that night." Her smile slowly faded. "I can't believe I ended up working for a marketing firm of all things." There was an inexplicable look in her eye that he thought might be regret. "Sometimes I want to go back to our college days, when it seemed like all it would take to get where we wanted to be was a piece of paper that said we had a degree. I miss that kind of sunny optimism."

"What if you get that promotion you've been talking about? Will you love your job then?"

"I'll be able to pay my bills every month, and I love the idea of that." She pulled her knees to her chest and folded her arms over the top. "It might not be my dream job, but I'm good at it, and I deserve to be promoted."

"I'm sure you do." He took in her profile, feeling a twinge of regret himself. "I just wish you didn't live so far away."

"Me, too. But maybe when I'm making more money, I'll be able to visit more often. And you being a pilot and all, I'm sure you could swing a few trips? When you're not too busy flying people to new adventures and being a rock star, of course."

"Oh, yes. In the one venue that the band regularly plays in because we know the owner, we're marginally more popular than the jukebox that plays hits from the seventies. My rock-star status is right around the corner." He leaned back on his hands, the tiny stones digging into his palms. "We're actually performing Saturday night—Audrey doesn't know I'm playing the night of her wedding or she'd kill me, but it's super late, so she'll never have to know."

"Finally, a show I can go to. I haven't heard you play with a band in years."

"Be prepared to be completely underwhelmed."

She laughed. She had the kind of infectious laugh that made him lighter and happier, even when he was feeling like crap. And for the first time in a long time, he didn't have to worry about the fact that his girlfriend would be pissed over his hanging out with Dani.

Being fake engaged to her was going to be a blast.

Chapter Two

Dani rolled her suitcase into Wes's apartment. A giant television lined one wall, there was a bookcase filled with video games, movies, and thick volumes on various wars, and he had one of those couches with the recliners and cup holders built in. But she couldn't believe how clean and organized the place was. His apartment in college had been a total hazard area, and the last time she'd visited here, the books and movies had been in stacks around the room along with half the clothes he owned.

"I *do* know how to clean," Wes said. Apparently he could read her mind. Or maybe her mouth was hanging open.

"Until now I really wasn't sure."

"Ha-ha." He stripped off his shirt, wadded it up, and shot it into the hallway. For a moment, she stared at his bare chest and abs. He must've been doing a lot of hiking. And ab-ing—'cause damn, you could wash laundry on that six-pack.

Then she felt weird about checking out his body. It wasn't like she'd never seen him shirtless before. They'd gone swimming, plus he sometimes took off his shirt while they hiked or played basketball. The fact he was in shape or good looking wasn't news. But damn, was he always in *that* good of shape?

She turned around, acting like she was still surveying the place. *It's just because I've been single for so long without so much as a date. And the guys in the office all have large guts and thinning hair.*

Certain her random hormone surge was under control now, she completed the circle she'd been slowly spinning, facing Wes again. He'd grabbed a bag of potato chips and a soda and flopped down on the couch. "You can shower first. There are fresh towels in the hall closet and my body wash will make you smell like a dude, but you're welcome to it. Anything else you need?"

"Nope. And I've got my own girly-smelling products, so I'm good." She rolled her suitcase to the bathroom, finding it as clean as the rest of the apartment.

Maybe some good came from his dating Sophie. Of course, his messiness never really bothered her to begin with.

After her shower, as she was blowing out her hair, she gave herself a pep talk. If she was becoming so desperate she was ogling her best friend, it was time for her to jump back into the dating scene. The pitiful part of her had been holding back, waiting for Steve to realize he missed her. But then more and more weeks passed, and the last time she'd sent him a pathetic how-are-things e-mail, he'd sent back one word: *fine.*

Two years together, a relocation for his job—that he ended up quitting to go back to college while she worked and paid all the bills—and in the end, she got dumped and one-word e-mail replies.

When I get back, I'm putting myself out there.

She lowered her hairdryer and frowned at her reflection. *How do I put myself out there when I have no friends to go out with?* She'd started working so much that she didn't have time to go out, and all the women at work were married. She just didn't have many other opportunities to meet people.

Well, however she had to do it, even if it meant putting up an online profile with one of those dating sites that wouldn't stop e-mailing her—not the cougar one, of course—she needed to do *something.*

She finished swiping her lashes with mascara, tossed the tube into her bag to punctuate the thought, and exited the bathroom. "Where should I tuck my suitcase? You care if it's out by the couch? I'd hate to ruin your chi."

"Oh, yeah. I'm big on my chi." Wes stepped into view, still shirtless, and pointed toward the closed door at the end of the hall. "You're staying in my bed."

His bed. All those muscles. Heat rose to her cheeks and she could feel her pulse steadily climbing. She couldn't seem to look away from the tattoo on his side. The thick black ink formed a tribal sun that morphed into a swirled shape with hints of a beak and wings, like a bird soaring away from the sun. She'd seen it before—she'd even been with him for one of the two sessions it'd taken to get it—yet her pulse was still climbing as she took in the way it cut off right where the V of his obliques led to his low-slung jeans. *Seriously, what's wrong with me?* She swallowed and it took way more effort than it should. "I love you and all, but I'm not sure I'm ready to be elbowed all night."

"I cleaned my room and even put fresh sheets on the bed so you could sleep there. I'll take the couch."

What was up with the squeeze of disappointment in her chest? She was just lonely; that had to be it. She missed having someone to cuddle up to at night. "You don't have to do that."

"Already done. Let me just grab my clothes." He took her suitcase handle but didn't move past her like she'd expected him to. He flicked the ends of her hair with his free hand. "I forgot how nice you look with your hair down."

If her mouth were working, she would've told him thanks. Offering her his bedroom *and* a compliment about her looks? This was a side of Wes she'd never seen. And she wasn't 100 percent sure how to handle it.

What she did know was she'd had more fun in the few hours she'd been in town than she'd had in the last few months combined.

• • •

The orange lights inside Whisky River illuminated Dani's dark hair. She turned to Wes, eyebrows drawn low. "What are we doing *here*? Did you go country and forget to tell me?"

"It's a fun place. And we're meeting Paul. Apparently Rob canceled—family emergency or something, although my guess is that his wife didn't want to come once she found out we were hanging out at this bar and grill."

A couple of guys walked by, running their eyes over Dani, and Wes found himself automatically doing the same. Years of basketball had toned her legs and arms, something her shorts and strappy top showed off. She was doing something different with her hair, too. A section of it hung halfway over her eye in this sexy way that had caught him a bit off guard when she'd stepped out of the bathroom earlier. He was sure even Paul, who'd recently sworn off women thanks to finding out his girlfriend was cheating on him, would reconsider his anti-woman stance when he met Dani.

She didn't seem to notice the guys, but she definitely noticed the mechanical bull at the front of the room. A girl was holding on, screeching as it bucked.

"Now it's all starting to make sense," Dani said.

The girl flew off the "bull," into the padding, her bleached-blond hair hanging over her face.

Wes worked to put on his most innocent expression. "I don't know what you're talking about. I come here for the onion rings and hot wings." He nudged her toward a table front and center where Paul was seated.

Wes introduced them as he and Dani slid into the cow-print booth. "Paul's going to help us pull off our scheme. He was about to propose to his girlfriend when they broke up, so he just so happens to have an extra diamond ring he's not using."

Paul hung his head and stared at a spot in the middle of the table. "I found out she was cheating on me, so… I keep telling myself I'm better off, but…"

Dani reached over and covered his hand with hers. "I'm so sorry." When it came to other people hurting, Dani was a total softie, the first to reach out and comfort someone, regardless of how well she knew him or her. "Bad breakups have happened to the best of us. Even Wes."

Okay, maybe not *that* soft. Her words jabbed him in the chest, leaving that annoying sting of rejection. If he were superstitious, he might've thought he and the band were cursed in love or something. But Rob's marriage seemed to be working just fine. He and his wife couldn't stop having babies, anyway.

Dani glanced down. "My last boyfriend left me. Not even for another woman, which is almost worse because it means he'd rather be alone than be with me."

It baffled Wes how hurt she sounded. Not because he didn't understand how that felt, but because she could do so much better.

"I was shocked by it, too," she said, shaking her head. "I think that makes it harder to get over. I guess when it comes to love, we're all kind of idiots, seeing the world with blinders."

"Love definitely made me stupid." Paul looked Dani over again. "Who'd dump you?"

"A total prick, that's who." Wes draped his arm over her shoulders. "You're better off without him."

She lifted her head. "I'm done with caring about Steve. I decided to move on."

Wes wished he felt ready to make that decision. He'd thought Sophie was the one, regardless of their differences, and the idea of starting over with someone new and going through all the inevitable relationship drama exhausted him. He didn't think Paul was ready, either—it'd been two months since he and Jennifer broke up, and it was still what he talked about more than not. All his "what if" questions made it harder for Wes to not think about the same thing with Sophie.

So back to the plan. Step one to getting over her included selling him and Dani as a legitimate couple. "Did you bring the ring?"

"I've been meaning to hawk it—at least try to get something back for it, but I…" Paul shrugged. He dug into his pocket, slowly pulled it out, and swallowed. "Anyway, here it is. Just be careful with it, dude."

Wes took the box from him. "I will. Just a couple of weeks, then I'll go with you to sell the damn thing." He was tempted to open up the box and look at the ring, but Paul was staring at it like an appendage he'd just lost.

Maybe this was a bad idea. Honestly, he'd hoped once Paul could see he was okay without the ring sitting there reminding him of what could've been, he'd feel better. Wes had certainly felt better when he'd gotten rid of Sophie's. It was a good first step to closure, anyway. Their food came, distracting them from their talk of stupid exes. Dani excused herself and Paul watched her head toward the bathroom.

"You guys are just pretending to be engaged, right?"

"Right," Wes said.

"But have you ever…? I mean, she's pretty and she seems nice…"

A smug satisfaction wound through him. "I thought all women were the devil. Wasn't that what you were saying earlier this week?"

"Well, most women. I'm not sure I'm ready to move on, but if I were..." Paul didn't say the rest. He didn't have to. What Wes was trying to figure out was if Dani and Paul would be good together. Honestly, he wanted her to find a nice guy, and his bandmate was a good guy. She might get a little bored with him but then again, obviously he had no clue how she chose guys. But the thought of her being with any guy bothered him—always had. No one ever appreciated her enough, and they took up her time, leaving less for him. Selfish, but true.

Of course, the hypothetical possibility of her and Paul didn't matter, because she didn't live here anymore. Unfortunately. Life would be so much better if his best friend didn't live so far away.

Dani came back to the table and stole a couple of onion rings from his plate as Wes glanced toward the mechanical bull no one had ridden since they'd gotten their food. "So, Paul thinks you should ride the bull."

She arched an eyebrow, an *oh really* expression on her face.

Paul held up his hands. "I didn't say that."

"But he's thinking it," Wes said. "And so am I. You've gotta try it at least once in your life."

She rolled her eyes. "Why? So all the guys can see my stuff bouncing around? No thanks."

"It's about the challenge of staying on."

"Mmm-hmm. I'm sure."

"If you ride, I'll ride. Then all the girls can watch my stuff bouncing around."

The corners of her mouth quivered, but she was working hard to keep the smile off her face. "You and all of your challenges. I'm too old for this stuff now."

"You're twenty-seven, not seventy."

She glared at him. "I have to pay for my hospital bills and insurance deductibles myself. If I get hurt, I'm screwed."

"So you're saying you don't have enough skills to not get hurt? The entire ring's padded."

She glanced at Paul, like he would be the voice of reason. Wes wouldn't have even known about this place if it weren't for him, so he knew she wasn't going to find it.

Paul shrugged. "Not saying you have to ride, but I'd definitely put my money on you."

Wes tossed an onion ring in his mouth and leaned back in his seat. "Five bucks I can ride longer than you."

She looked from him to the bull and then back at him. "You go first."

Challenge accepted—he knew she'd cave. Excitement zipping through his stomach, he stood. He tipped an imaginary cowboy hat at her. "In all fairness, darlin', I should probably warn you that this ain't my first rodeo."

She laughed and swiped her hand through the air. "Less talk, more walk, cowboy."

He leaned over her, took one last swig of his drink, and charged toward the front. Yes, he'd been to a rodeo before, when he was really little. At one point, he'd even told his mom he wanted to be a bull rider—she'd been quick to stomp that one out. But he'd never come close to actually riding a bull. At least this one wouldn't charge after him or trample him when he fell.

He kicked off his shoes, like the guy working the bull told him to, and a loud whistle came from the audience. Dani did this fingers-in-the-mouth whistle thing that could practically deafen anyone in near proximity. He bowed and then climbed on. A couple of other women had lined up to watch and he shot them a big grin. One blonde was kind of cute. Maybe if he didn't make a fool of himself, he'd go chat her up.

Wes gripped the rope and the rocking started. The thing bounced more than bucked. Usually it started out slow, but the guy must've cranked it up. It started spinning faster and faster, going up and down harder, whipping him back and forth. Making his back crack.

I just gotta hold on longer than Dani can.

His fingers slipped, and then he was on his butt on the padded mat. The red numbers above the ring read forty-seven seconds. By the time he got his shoes back on, Dani was slipping hers off, getting ready to go.

"I can't believe I'm doing this," she muttered.

"Would now be a bad time to admit that the bouncing *is* most of the allure?" He winked because he knew it would make her crazy. On cue, two bright spots of red showed on her cheeks and her jaw clenched.

Then her eyes lit up and something deep inside his gut stirred. "You must be scared if you're trying to get me to change my mind," she said.

He took a step closer and echoed her words from earlier. "Less talk, more walk, cowgirl."

Her mouth dropped and then she charged past him into the ring. Wes leaned against the edge of the railing, chuckling to himself.

The two girls, including the cute blonde, scooted closer to him.

"It's so cool that you rode it. The guys usually don't."

About a minute ago, he'd wanted to talk to the girl who was smiling at him and twirling her hair around her finger. Now he was focused on Dani, thinking he hadn't had this much fun in months. He'd forgotten how fired up she got when he implied she couldn't do something. As she climbed on the bull, though, he noticed all the guys in the place leaning forward, pervy looks on their faces, and started wondering if getting her up there was a mistake.

Keep your eyes to yourself, he wanted to growl at them all. But then the guy working the bull asked if she was ready, and he couldn't really talk, because he was staring right along with the rest of them.

• • •

Now that Dani was straddling the mechanical bull, her palms were sweating and she was questioning her decision to tell the guy to put it on the same level he'd used for Wes.

All she had to do was rock with it instead of fight against it. Right? She focused all her thoughts toward holding on, squeezing her thighs around the contraption and trying in vain not to think about how her boobs would be jiggling for everyone to see.

With a screech, the beast lunged, bouncing in a way she doubted a real bull would. She gritted her teeth and closed her eyes; it was easier to feel the movements that way. Moving the way she'd seen cowboys on TV ride bulls—well, all of one time ever, when she'd been staring more at how cute the guys were than the riding—she thought this wasn't so bad.

Then the movements got faster. More bouncing. Wishing for a sports bra. Fingers slipping.

Shit.

She tumbled off the side onto her back. Although riding the thing couldn't be much cardio, she was breathing heavily like she'd just run, her heart thumping fast. She quickly rolled over to see her time.

Happiness bubbled up in her. Forty-nine seconds.

She'd take it.

As she made her way to where Wes was standing, it felt like the ground under her feet was still moving. "Okay, that was fun. And I'm not just saying that because I beat you, which I did, in case you hadn't noticed."

It took Wes a few seconds longer than usual to smile.

"Everything cool?" she asked.

He ran a hand through his hair and swallowed, his Adam's apple slowly moving up and down. "Super cool."

She noticed two girls just down from Wes and leaned in. "Those girls are checking you out."

"They were totally objectifying me while I was riding the bull, too." He rubbed a hand across his chest. "I feel so violated."

Dani rolled her eyes but couldn't help smiling. "Yeah, I'm sure you weren't eating up every second of the attention." She leaned in conspiratorially. "The blonde even looks like your type. Why don't you get her number?"

"I seem to remember you being annoyed in college when I got a girl's number and didn't call. False hope or something."

"So call her."

He glanced at the blonde and she beamed at him. Dani should probably be offended the girl was flirting so blatantly with him when, for all she knew, Dani could be his girlfriend. He gave the chick a small smile, then turned back to her. "I'm good."

He jerked his head toward the table and they started back. "So how long am I going to have to hear about how you beat my time?"

"Oh, probably forever."

"Do I need to remind you who won the dance-off in college?"

"A *video-game* dance-off, and I still think my machine wasn't reading my stomps right. I rule at dancing."

They settled back at the table.

"So what about you, Paul?" Dani asked. "You going to see if you can beat my or Wes's time?" She lifted a hand and stage-whispered, "Mine was better, in case you didn't see."

Paul shook his head. "I think I'll sit this one out. Probably all the other ones, too, actually."

Dani smiled at him, and he returned it. She glanced at Wes, and he offered her the last onion ring without her even having to ask. She took it and leaned back, soaking in the buzz from riding the "bull" and being out actually doing something. It made her think that her new goal of getting back out there—back into the dating game—was a good one. She'd been just floating through life for far too long, and being around Paul and Wes gave her hope that maybe there were still good guys out there. She'd doubted it recently, but it was good to know. The question was, were there any in Arkansas? And how was she going to meet them if there were?

Wes glanced at his phone. "Hey, if we're going to pull off this engagement thing, we better go drop the bomb on my family."

Chapter Three

Wes's phone chirped as he and Dani pushed out of the restaurant. It was a text from Audrey, recommending a good hairdresser. He rolled his eyes. Audrey was the girlier one of his sisters by far, and she was crazy bossy over all the wedding stuff. In the end he'd shave and get his hair trimmed, just so he didn't have to hear how he'd ruined her special day—and okay, because it'd make her happy—but he was going to torture her by not giving in quite yet.

She immediately sent a follow-up text asking if he'd had his suit dry cleaned yet and when he was going to be at Mom and Dad's, because they were all waiting for him, and she needed everyone there so she could go over the pre-wedding schedule for the next few days.

Weddings. What a pain in the ass. And to think if things had gone differently, he and Sophie would be getting married in a month. A strange mixture of regret and relief rolled through him.

He shook off those thoughts, turning them to what he and Dani were about to announce. He'd talked about her enough that his family all knew who she was, and Audrey had even met her before, a few years back. If it weren't for that, they'd probably tell him it was too fast to be engaged again. Just like they'd been telling him for the last three months that he should try to move on.

As Wes rounded the hood of his car, he sent a text back saying that he was on his way, purposely leaving out that he was bringing someone.

"Ready for the craziness?" he asked as he settled behind the wheel.

Dani swiped her hair behind her ear and it immediately fell forward again. "Well, when you put it like that…"

"You'll be fine. My family's going to love you." Now to put the final touch on his plan. He took the ring box Paul had given him out of his pocket. The streetlight caught the diamond as Wes lifted the ring. It was much bigger than the one he'd given Sophie, and he was sure when she saw it, she'd take note.

"Talk about a rock," Dani said. "Five bucks your family notices it before we can officially announce anything."

Wes tossed the box into his center console, keeping the ring pinched between his fingers. "You're on. But no flashing it or it doesn't count." Not that money ever exchanged hands anymore. They bet five dollars over everything, but they both won and lost so often, it was just assumed they broke even.

Dani extended her hand, and he was pretty sure it was trembling a bit. His fingers were shaking, too, and his throat was suddenly dry. Maybe it was because he'd done this before and it'd gone to hell, or maybe he'd turned into more of a commitment phobe than he wanted to admit. If he felt nervous slipping it on Dani's finger, he didn't want to think of how bad it would be if this were for real.

The ring took a little work to get over her knuckle, but then she lifted her hand in front of her face and stared at the diamond, scrunching up her nose.

"What?" he asked.

"I don't know. It's just…odd. To have it on my finger. This whole thing." She looked at him through the fringe of hair hanging over one of her eyes. "Are you sure this isn't crazy?"

"Oh, I'm sure it *is* crazy. But isn't that our thing? Or have you gotten boring now?"

That defiant expression that meant she'd not only go along but also go all out crossed her face—man, he loved goading her. "You better strap yourself in, Wes Turner. I'm not sure you can handle being engaged to me."

Already this was way more fun than it should be. "Bring it on, *sweetheart*. But remember, you have to act like you're in love with me."

She raised an eyebrow. "If you think I'm the doting kind of girlfriend, you've got another thing coming."

"And when they ask why I fell for you, that's exactly what I'll say." He lifted his chin. "Well, you see, she's kind of mean and tells me I look like Paul Bunyan and a hobo. How could I *not* fall for that?"

"Then I'll say, but despite all those things, once I learned he was a pilot and heard him play guitar"—she threw a hand over her heart and gave a dramatic sigh—"I was a goner. That and his crystal clear blue eyes, of course."

Wes started the car and readjusted his rearview mirror. "Don't forget my rock-hard body."

"And your humility."

He laughed. Over the phone they always joked around, but having her here in person was a hundred times better. If there had been any romantic chemistry between them at all, he'd propose for real, just so they wouldn't have to live so far apart anymore.

His mind flashed to the image of her riding that bull, moving against it. He'd been unable to look away the entire forty-nine seconds, his heart pounding in his chest like it was about to explode, thinking about things he *so* shouldn't be thinking about.

Suppress that image, Turner. Never happening. While there was no denying it'd been much hotter watching his best friend ride that bull than he'd expected, there was a difference between attraction and romantic chemistry.

And as he and Dani had learned one hazy mistake of a night, that was a line they were better off staying far, far away from.

A short drive later, they pulled up to his parents' house in Huntersville.

"Whoa," Dani said, peering up at the three-story stone and brick house, eyes wide. He'd grown up on the other side of town in a much smaller home, so he still wasn't fully used to it, either.

"After my dad sold his business, they bought this place." If she thought the front was impressive, she'd be floored when she saw the grounds out back, especially after all the wedding preparations. Honestly, it struck him as ridiculous to do so much landscaping for a ceremony and celebration that would last a couple of hours, but voicing that to Mom or Audrey would earn him the Look of Death.

Wes got out of the car and met Dani in front of the hood. "So, do we hold hands when we go up or...?"

She shrugged. "You're the one who's done this before, not me."

"Well, at least you don't rub it in or anything."

"I'm sure it's one of our biggest fights now that we're engaged." Her dark eyebrows drew together. "Girls pick fights over that stuff, right?"

The reason why Dani had always been practically one of the guys was that she didn't act like most girls. Not only did she like the same things he liked, she also told him exactly how she felt—blunt to the point of being harsh sometimes. In fact, if he didn't clarify that she was a girl when he talked about her, people assumed she was Danny, a guy. "Girls can pick fights over anything, I've found."

She gave one sharp nod. "Got it. Pick little fights to show everyone we're legit." She cracked her knuckles and neck. That noise always made his own joints hurt. They just weren't supposed to pop like that. "Now hold my freakin' hand and let's do this."

"Geez, you want to throw our hands together and yell out, 'Go team!' too? Relive the glory days playing college basketball?"

"Ah yes, the glory days when I worked my butt off and constantly got yelled at by my coach. Good times, good times."

The curtains moved, and Wes had a feeling his arrival—and the fact that he was with someone—was being announced throughout the house. His family was the nosy type, always in one another's business, expressing their opinions even when you didn't ask. But that was why they were so close, too, with frequent family get-togethers filled with stories and good-natured teasing.

Introducing his entire family to Dani was long overdue, something he would've done for sure if she hadn't moved to Arkansas. He'd never planned for it to go down quite like this, though.

He grabbed Dani's hand. They stumbled for a second, not sure whether to go with the simple hand clasp or fingers intertwined. "Shit, we're bad at this."

She laughed. "I'm rusty, but I expected you to be smoother after all your experience with the band groupies."

"I do not go for groupies, thank you very much." Wes clamped onto her hand, forgetting about trying to lace their fingers, and dragged her toward the front door. His heart beat faster and he couldn't help but smile at how crazy this night was going to be. He probably should've prepped Dani for the fact that his extended family was going to be here, too, but it'd be so much more fun this way.

"Five bucks my mom offers you a guest room after she finds out about the engagement, so that we're not sleeping in my apartment together."

"I'll just tell her we're waiting," Dani said. "Five bucks she likes me more than you by the end of the night."

Wes opened the door, grinning when people scurried away like cockroaches from a light, trying to pretend they hadn't just been hovering around the door watching him and Dani. All but his nephew and niece. They charged.

"Uncle Wes!" they cried out, wrapping themselves around his legs.

He let go of Dani's hand to hug them as his sisters came into the room with their significant others. Grandma Turner entered the foyer, his uncles, aunts, and cousins close behind her. Mom came out of the kitchen, wiping her hands on her apron, the sweet scent of whatever she was baking following her.

All eyes slowly moved to Dani.

She reached for his hand, and he felt a little guilty for not warning her just how huge his family was. The deer in the headlights look reminded him that she was an only child.

He squeezed her hand. "Hope nobody minds, but I brought along a guest for dinner." Audrey stepped forward. "Dani, hi! I almost didn't recognize you."

Murmurs went through his entire family, a variety of "Who's Dani?" and "That's her?"

Audrey's eyes shot to the ring on Dani's finger and her

mouth dropped. Wes meant to wait—but Dani had been right about them noticing the diamond. No way he was going to let his sister blurt it out, like he could see she was about to.

"Everyone, I'd like you to meet Danielle Vega. My fiancée."

. . .

Dani inched closer to Wes. So much for waiting until she'd met everyone before announcing their engagement. She should've known he couldn't wait—*impulsive* was his middle name. Usually it was what she loved about him, but now she had...she didn't even know how many people staring at her, like they expected an explanation. At least none of them looked appalled.

"You're engaged?" Audrey shook her head, turned around, and stormed out of the room.

Okay, so apparently she's *appalled.*

The lady wearing an apron looked from Wes to Dani. Then she threw her hands over her mouth and tears gathered in her eyes.

Dani pulled back, ready to bolt back out the door.

A high-pitched squeal came from the woman and then she was rushing forward and hugging Wes. She slung one arm around Dani, too—the woman was surprisingly strong. That seemed to be some kind of signal for everyone else to do the same, and soon Dani was being hugged and congratulated by people whose names she still didn't know.

Wes started pointing and telling her names she desperately tried to assign to faces. This wasn't the intimate dinner with his parents and siblings she'd envisioned when he'd brought up this plan.

As soon as she had a couple of inches of personal space back, she leaned into Wes and whispered, "I don't know how yet, but I'm so going to get you back for this."

Wes grinned. "Aw, thanks, hon. I love you so much, too."

I'm going to kill him. I'm actually going to kill him.

Wes's mother—Kathy or Kathleen, Dani couldn't remember—patted Wes on the shoulder. "Could you go help your dad and uncles set up the table and chairs outside?"

Dani tightened her grip on Wes's hand. "I'll help, too."

His mother grabbed her other hand. "It's okay, dear. The boys will get it. You come chat with us girls. I've recently become an expert on weddings, and we should start talking about yours as soon as possible." She tugged Dani toward the kitchen. After one quick glance at Wes, who had an amused smile on his face, she reluctantly followed.

A moment later, she found herself in a room full of girls. Wes's older sister, Jill, and some nameless aunts and cousins were huddled around Audrey. As soon as she looked up, though, she stood and gave Dani a tight smile. "I'm sorry; I was just so shocked. It's good to see you again." She ran her French-manicured nails through her perfectly highlighted blond hair. "So how'd this happen?"

Heat crawled up Dani's neck into her cheeks. When it came to being out on the gym floor, she loved the spotlight. Without a ball in her hand and only her conversational skills to rely on, though, she couldn't help but squirm under the scrutiny. "How'd what happen?"

"Hello? You and Wes are engaged! For years I've heard over and over again, 'We're just friends.'"

The other women in the room nodded.

Crap. She and Wes should've discussed this. Why hadn't they thought up a good story? That was the problem with them both jumping in without fully thinking things through. She figured the more truth she could weave in, the better. "Well, I've always loved Wes."

A collective sigh went through the room.

"But we recently realized we needed each other, and things sort of progressed from there."

"Tell us about how he proposed," Jill said, scooting forward in her chair.

Yet another story we should've come up with. Something told her they weren't looking for *He gave me an almost-used ring in his car after bull riding at Whiskey River.* "Um, we went for a hike. We stopped to look over the valley, and Wes pulled out the ring and asked me." Yeah. That sounded okay. And they'd been on a hike recently, so that worked—not that she thought anyone would be demanding evidence.

She hoped.

"What were his exact words?" Kathy—no, Kathleen, she was almost sure—asked.

"Just, um, 'Will you marry me?'"

More sighs.

Kathleen patted her hand. "And, honey, where are you staying right now? Because we have plenty of room here, and we'd be happy to have you. I could fix you up a guest room tonight."

If Wes asked, she was denying this ever happened. All bets were off the instant he shoved her into this craziness. When Kathleen raised her eyebrows and tilted her head, Dani said, "Thank you so much for the offer, but I'm staying with Wes." Before his mom could insist she stay here and her supposed-to-be-relaxing vacation went to hell, she turned to Audrey. "So, you're getting married in three days! That's so exciting."

Pretty soon the conversation was about flowers and dresses and everything they still needed to get done before Saturday.

Even though Wes's family was huge, and nothing like hers, it made her miss her own family. After her father passed away when she was ten, she and Mama had to pull together and keep getting through life one day at a time. Abuela Morales had visited often to help out, and they'd all kept one another going through the years. When Abuela's health started slipping, Mama moved in with her to help out. It'd been forever since Dani had visited, and if Mama or Abuela even got wind of this engagement, fake or not, she'd never hear the end of it.

I should call and check in. See if Abuela is still trying to take off her oxygen, claiming she doesn't need the stuff. It was expensive to have it in-home, but breathing was vital to life, so it was staying, no matter how much Abuela fought it. *It'd be so much easier if she'd stop resisting the things she needs to get better.*

"Dani?"

She jerked out of her thoughts, looking toward the voice. Kathleen. "Sorry, what was that?"

"Have you and Wes picked a date or location?"

Luckily, Wes chose that moment to poke his head into the room. "The backyard's set up and Dad took out the dessert and wine already," he said. "Let's all go hear what the boss wants us to do the rest of the week." He flashed a smile at Audrey, who stuck her tongue out at him.

Dani quickly stood and moved over to him. She wanted to stay mad, but he winked at her, a goofy grin on his face. As much as she teased him about the scruff, it did look pretty hot on him. She wondered if it'd be weird if she ran her fingers down it again—she could always play it off as part of the engaged act, after all.

Wes put his hand on the small of her back. "So did Dani tell you about how I proposed to her at my show, in front of an entire audience?"

Confusion flickered across all the faces in the room.

She slid her arm around his waist. "I told them how you asked me after we took a hike. Out in nature."

"Right! The first proposal. That was the real one, of course. Then I called her out of the audience at our show to embarrass her."

No one sighed. *Ha. They like my story better.*

Gradually, everyone got up and headed outside. At the top of the porch steps, Wes grabbed her elbow, holding her back. "I didn't plan on announcing it, but you were right about the ring being noticeable. How'd it go with the girls? Audrey didn't make you feel bad, did she? She's been moody for weeks, so whatever her deal is, it has nothing to do with you."

"Next thing you know, you'll be telling me that failing to mention your entire freakin' family was going to be here had nothing to do with you."

"Oh, that was all me." His grin widened. "Thought it'd be more fun."

She was considering shoving him down the steps for *fun*, but then she noticed all of his family was suddenly watching them with weird expressions on their faces.

"Um, why's everyone—"

"Dani?" she heard from behind her, and Wes tensed.

She wouldn't have recognized the voice, but from Wes's reaction, she was pretty sure she knew who'd be there. Sure enough, Sophie stood just behind them. "I needed to ask Audrey a quick question about the shoes..." She held up a bag. "I didn't realize... I mean, I knew *you*'d be here." She glanced at Wes. "But I didn't expect... Sorry. Hi, Dani."

A breeze blew Dani's hair in her face and she reached up to tuck it behind her ear.

Sophie gasped and her face paled. Her gaze was glued to the ring on Dani's finger. "Did you and Steve get back together?" There was a sad, hopeful pinch to her voice.

Wes slid his arm around Dani's waist. She tried to remind herself this was why she'd come, and that Sophie was the one who'd dumped Wes, but there was a sick, heavy feeling in her gut instead of the "so there" victorious high she'd expected.

"Dani and I are...engaged," Wes said.

"Oh. Well." Sophie's smile was more like a grimace. "Congratulations." She raised her voice and glanced at where everyone was sitting, watching the show. "Audrey, can I steal you away for a second?"

Under normal circumstances, Dani would be mentally mocking her for saying, *Can I steal you?* But right now she was too busy feeling sorry for her.

She doesn't have a right to be hurt, though. If she wanted Wes, she shouldn't have crushed him. She deserves to feel stupid for letting him go.

Wes was putting on a cool front, but Dani could feel his fingers twitching at her waist and see the uncomfortable pinch to his features. There was a whole lot of awkwardness coming at her from the entire family, actually. And Dani wondered, once again, if Wes were actually as over his ex as he claimed.

Chapter Four

Wes glanced over his shoulder at Dani when he heard her footsteps. He grated cheese onto the eggs and slid a plate across the counter to her.

Her eyelids were still half closed and she was shuffling more than walking—she wasn't a morning person and would actually get mad at him when he was happy first thing, often asking *what his deal was*. It was kind of cute, this messy hair, scrunched-together eyebrows, and lips-stuck-out-in-a-pout side of her.

"You think breakfast is all it takes to make me forget you threw me to the wolves last night?" she asked.

"One, those wolves are my family. And two, you haven't tried my eggs yet. This super-smart girl taught me to put green chilies and cheese in them." He shot her an extra-sugary grin and extended a fork.

She stared at it for a moment and then swiped it out of his hand. "You're lucky I'm hungry."

He sat across from her and dug into his breakfast. "I think last night went pretty well, actually. Now that my family knows about the engagement, the hardest part is over. Hopefully they'll leave me alone from here on out."

"No, they're going to want to know when and where and a hundred other details." She shook her head. "I should've known you'd make up an onstage proposal."

"What's wrong with that? As if a proposal after a hike really sounds like me."

"Hey, I was on the spot because of you." She pointed her fork at him, a dangerous look in her eye. "If we're going to really do this, we need to get our stories straight."

He leaned his forearms on the table. "If? One night with my family was enough to scare you off?"

"Not your family. Sophie. It seemed like…" She stirred her eggs with her fork, the scraping noise against her plate loud in the sudden quiet.

Wes tensed. "Like what?"

"Like there are some unresolved issues there."

He gripped the counter so that the edge dug into his palms, not wanting to get into this. "I'm resolving the issue. I'm engaged to you now."

She tilted her head, giving him that no-nonsense look. He usually liked that she called him on his crap, but sometimes—like now—it was annoying. "Seems like delaying the issue to me. Look, I know you're a guy—"

"Damn straight."

"And there's some man rule that you've got to be all macho—"

"Rule number three, actually."

Both of her eyebrows shot up. "Would you just let me finish before I make you cry and break *rule number three*?"

He considered telling her to go ahead and try, but clamped his lips instead. When she set her mind to something, there wasn't much chance of changing it, so he might as well ride it out and be done with it.

"Don't give me that face. I'm not saying we need to have a big talk about it, but as someone who was dumped by the guy I thought was the one, I do understand, you know. You hate the person and still want to get back together somehow, even though it makes no logical sense. It sucks and it hurts and you want to return the hurt right back. But are you sure this fake engagement thing isn't going to make things worse?"

Wes sighed. Time and time again, his sisters had asked him what went wrong, how he felt, a hundred other questions that he didn't want to answer. But Dani was here and, unlike his sisters, she did get it. He was pissed she was pushing him, yet glad at the same time. He wanted to get how he'd felt the last few months off his chest. "Ever since we broke up, I've felt lost, trying to figure out what I really want. And I still don't have a damn clue. But I do know that I need to prove to her, to my family, and to myself that I can move on."

He reached across the counter and grabbed Dani's hand. "So yes, I still want to go through with our plan. It feels like finally closing that chapter in my life, and hopefully after this wedding everyone will stop asking me about Sophie and what happened, and I can move on for real."

She stared back at him, unblinking for a moment, then squeezed his hand. "Okay. If you think it'll help you. I just don't want to be the thing that gets in between you and Sophie resolving whatever…" She made a vague hand motion, like she didn't know how to finish.

It was a nice thought, but it didn't change anything. Besides, regardless of what everyone seemed to think, he didn't want to be with Sophie anymore. He truly just wanted to get on with his life and look into the helicopter tour idea more seriously.

He stood to dump his dish in the sink, and Dani came over to do the same. He filled a glass with orange juice and handed it to her. While he was serious about putting his past behind him, he wasn't sure Dani actually was, despite what she'd said last night. "Since we're talking about this stuff, what are you doing to move on from Steve the Prick?" When she didn't say anything, he added, "Not so fun now that you're the one having to talk about your ex, is it?"

"I'm trying, okay? But it's not like anyone's asked me out."

"I think you've got to go places besides work for that to happen."

She shot him a glare.

"Plus, you can be kind of intimidating."

She blew out her breath, making a *pfft* noise with her lips. "Me? Intimidating? That's the stupidest thing I've ever heard."

"See what I mean? You don't soften anything. I try to tell you something, and you call me stupid."

"Well, you've stuck through my not softening anything all these years."

"Yeah, but I'm not trying to date you."

She leaned back against the counter and her T-shirt rode up a few inches, showing off a stripe of her toned stomach. Guys in Arkansas must be blind or stupid. "Yesterday I was thinking it was time to get out there again, but today I'm wondering why I should bother. It's kind of nice to be unattached. To visit you without having to defend myself the whole time." She lifted one shoulder. "Maybe being single for a while wouldn't be the worst thing in the world."

Wes took a gulp of orange juice straight from the carton, something that used to drive Sophie crazy, and wiped his mouth with the back of his hand. "You might be on to something."

"And maybe we'll know we've found the right person when we're with people who are actually cool enough to accept us for who we are." She bumped her shoulder against his. "And who our best friend happens to be."

He tapped the carton to her glass. "Cheers to that. Now let's put all this behind us and have some fun."

"What did you have in mind?"

• • •

Dani should've known from the smile Wes had flashed her earlier that she was in trouble. But she'd gone along with the "it's a surprise" answer, foolishly thinking it'd be a fun adventure. Now her throat was dry as she studied the red helicopter. She'd never told anyone, but she always hated that moment before taking off in an airplane. And even worse, when the plane was heading toward the ground and the bumpy landing she always feared would turn into a fiery crash. Those were the times she'd muttered desperate prayers.

Riding in a helicopter with Wes the adrenaline junkie at the controls? She didn't know if there was a prayer big enough.

He put his hand on her arm. "If I didn't know any better, I'd think you were second-guessing going for a ride with me."

"You can't second-guess if you never once guessed." She took a step back from the machine. "You go fly around for a few minutes and I'll meet up with you later."

He caught her hand as she tried to take another step back. "You're the one who told me I'd be good at this. Don't you trust me?"

She glanced from him to the helicopter and swallowed, but there was still a big knot in her throat.

"It was bad enough when you talked me into that bungee jump thing at Carowinds Amusement Park right after graduation. And while I was screaming and my life was flashing before my eyes, you told me you thought my harness was slipping."

He clamped his mouth, but she could tell he was fighting a smile. "I'll take it easy." He pulled her toward the aircraft. She tried dragging her feet, but it wasn't slowing him down like she hoped it would.

When they got to the door of the helicopter, Wes gestured her inside. She looked at the seat but didn't make a move to get in.

"Do I have to throw you inside and strap you down?" he asked.

"You wouldn't dare."

"Wanna put five bucks on it?" Amusement flickered through his eyes.

"It's not funny, Wes. I didn't want to admit this, but flying freaks me out."

"Dani. We've rock climbed, ridden down intense rapids, gone scuba diving, and you're scared of *flying*?"

She scuffed her foot on the landing pad. "It's bad enough in a big airplane, where I wouldn't really see the ground coming at me if the plane went down. But there's not as much crash room and I'd be able to see everything, and I never would've done those other things without you daring me to, but at least the worst-case scenarios didn't involve falling from the sky and dying a fiery death." Her stomach clenched as gory scenes flashed through her mind.

"I'm not going to crash us. I do this several times a day."

She waited for the hard-to-resist dare—calling her a wuss or a girl or all the other tricks he'd used before to convince her to let go of her common sense and do something stupid. His fingers grazed her chin and then he gently tipped her face up to his.

"The constantly moving rotor makes it easier for me to maneuver than any plane. Also, there's no wind today, so it's perfect weather, and I want to show you the most amazing view of Charlotte, one you've never seen before. I promise you, we'll come back safe and sound. But I won't force you inside."

She looked into his pale blue eyes, and something twisted inside of her. She wasn't sure exactly what it meant, but she knew she was getting into his stupid helicopter despite her gut-wrenching fear.

She let out a long exhale. "Okay."

"I knew you'd see reason," he said, and the maddening touch of arrogance made her reach out and flick his shoulder. His cocky grin only widened.

She glanced up at the cloudless blue sky they were about to be flying into, took a deep breath of humid air, and climbed inside. Unable to relax, she sat with her back straight up and gnawed on her lip. Her fingers trembled as she put on the seat belt, checking the clasp three times.

Like it'll save me if we go down anyway. Her pulse spiked. *Don't think about that, don't think about that.*

Wes got in and flipped all kinds of switches. A low hum vibrated the cabin and then the whoosh of the rotors overhead picked up speed, growing louder and louder. "Just don't touch any of the handles or buttons and keep your feet away from the pedals. You're not quite ready to co-pilot yet." He said it like a joke, but she so wasn't finding it funny. He handed her earphones and practically had to yell now. "These cut the noise but still allow us to talk to each other."

She put them on, feeling like a dork. They were seriously huge.

Wes slid on a pair of aviator shades. Even with the headphones, he managed to look cool. His scruff wasn't so long that his jaw line got lost in it, he'd gelled his hair so the waves were still messy but more defined, and the gray button-down he wore had the top few buttons undone and the sleeves casually pushed up so the sun glinted off the blond hair on his forearms. In fact, there was something about his whole look, sitting in the pilot's seat, shades on, that made him ten times hotter, even though she was pretty sure he was about to crash them both into the side of a mountain.

First the eyes, now I'm thinking about his hotness again? She really must be about to die, because those were not the kind of thoughts she should be having right now.

"Ready?" he asked.

She gripped the edges of her seat. "How long did you train for this again?"

He laughed, and she was going to ask if he was purposely avoiding answering, but then they were lifting into the air and her stomach was rising, and, *oh shit!* What was she thinking getting into a flying vehicle with an adrenaline junkie? It'd been a long time since she'd done anything more dangerous than go on blind dates set up by her coworkers.

Her mom and abuela relied on her; she had a job, bills, and responsibilities to think about. She didn't have the luxury of being daring or living on the edge anymore—or more like being pushed onto the edge by Wes. Maybe it was better that they didn't live close to each other anymore.

The buildings and trees got smaller and smaller and her heart beat faster and harder. Wes was pushing his feet and moving levers. There were so many dials and gauges that she clenched her hands into fists just to be sure she didn't accidentally bump something and make them crash.

"The back rotor moves with the foot pedals." He demonstrated and they swayed from side to side a bit. "Pull up on this and we climb higher."

Her stomach climbed higher right along with them.

"Don't forget to breathe," he said.

"Right. Breathing." Easier said than done.

"See the city?"

The tall uptown buildings jutted into the skyline. She could make out the blue seats in the Bank of America

Stadium where the Panthers played. Her heart was jumping all over the place, her rushing blood thrumming through her head. If they went down, she was going to have a front-row seat to the ground coming at her.

Her stomach lurched, and she was worried she might lose her breakfast. *It's such a long fall. And we'd definitely crash into something solid, the kind of fiery, parts-flying-everywhere crash in the action movies.*

"Tell me how Charlotte got its name," Wes said. When she didn't answer after a moment, he nudged her. "Dani. Tell me."

She glanced at him. "You know how."

"Humor me. I'll do the flying, you pretend you're doing the tour."

She closed her eyes, focusing on the facts. "It was named for the queen consort of King George the third. Which is why it's sometimes called the Queen City. It also used to be known as the city of churches, but now it's known as a major US financial center, thus the stadium named after a bank."

"Perfect. I should hire you to be my tour guide, so I don't have to do all the talking. You've got a better voice for it." He pointed. "You know what that building is?"

She opened her eyes to see what he was referencing. "Is that the Levine Museum that we went to when we were writing our Post Civil War paper?"

"Yep."

Her eyes moved past the museum to the other buildings, trying to place them. The scary details faded away as she took in all the tiny little squares of different colors laid out in an intricate patchwork of buildings, parking lots, the swirl of the freeway with all the tiny cars, and, off in the distance, the city dissolving into a sea of green trees. Then she noticed how blue the sky was, the tiny cotton clouds stretched all around. Her breath actually caught in her throat at how beautiful the view truly was from up here.

That was when she realized the heaviness in her chest had lifted and her heart rate had returned to normal. She smiled at Wes, who was watching her take it all in with a big grin on his face. It was crazy how well he knew her, how he always found a way to push her to do things yet make her see past the fear and enjoy it. "Nice trick."

"You're not thinking about the fact you might plummet to your death anymore, are you?"

She'd smack him if she wasn't worried that it'd cause a crash. "Thanks for putting that image back in my mind," she said, but the fear was completely gone, replaced by a lightness, like she'd left all her cares on the ground. And she found she did trust Wes to get them wherever they were going safely.

He flashed her another smile and then they were flying across the city, buildings and streets a blur beneath them. He buzzed over to Wingate University, where they'd met. She wondered if any of the barely visible people down there were meeting someone for the first time. Someone who might turn into their best friend—someone who would make them go on crazy adventures they'd never dare try alone.

Dani leaned forward, warmth filling her as she thought of her and Wes's days on campus. "If only I could go back in time and warn my past self of all the trouble her charming new study buddy was going to get her into."

"You still wouldn't have been able to stay away from me," Wes said. "Admit it—I make your life more fun."

"Fun. Dangerous. All of the above." Truthfully, she always liked who she was when she was around Wes. She laughed more and was more spontaneous and funnier and all the things she wished she could be without him but just wasn't. And now that she was up in the air, she was glad he'd talked her into coming.

"I saved the best for last." He angled the helicopter back

toward Charlotte and they buzzed around the outskirts of the city. Underneath them was a blur of green trees until Lake Norman came into view.

He looked at her like he was waiting for her reaction. Funny enough, she always felt safer when planes were over an ocean or lake, like the water would envelop her if she fell instead of tenderizing her body.

The sun glittered off the lake's surface. Tiny boats were leaving white trails in the water. "It's beautiful." Beautiful in a way that wrapped her in peace and gave her the kind of spiritual calm that people talked about feeling in church. It was a picture on the wall, one of those paintings that you want to take home so you never have to leave the place. Only it was real.

I can't believe I almost missed this.

Wes patted her knee. "See? Not scary at all, and I totally know what I'm doing. You feel safe now, right?

"Yeah. I do," she said, and she was surprised at how true it was. "I'm glad you talked me into coming." All her warm fuzzies disappeared as a wicked grin curved his lips. "Wes, no. Whatever you're thinking about doing, just—"

The *don't* was left somewhere behind her as the helicopter dove toward the water.

• • •

After this, Dani might not want to ride with him ever again, but he couldn't help himself. He aimed down, toward the lake, watching her eyes fly wide.

"Wes…" She grabbed his arm. Her grip tightened as they got closer to the surface. "Wes!"

Last minute, he brought them back up, the landing skids grazing the water. She punched his shoulder. "Jerk."

"Come on. It was a *little* fun."

She tried to hold her dirty look, but she never could keep one for long. "I hope it was fun for you, because as soon as we're on solid ground again, I'm going to kill you. And I'd feel bad if you hadn't enjoyed your last few hours on earth."

He poked her in the side, knowing it drove her crazy. "If I had a dollar for every time you'd threatened to kill me, I'd be able to buy my own plane by now."

She smacked his hand, but the corners of her mouth couldn't hold her serious expression anymore. A slight dimple he'd never noticed before came out in her cheek. "I hope you do get your own helicopter someday to do your adventure tours, but the only way I'm going on one is if the Holy Grail is at the end. And I'm making you drink out of it first to make sure it doesn't melt skin off bones."

"Deal." He tipped the nose of the helicopter up, lifting them higher in the air.

When they'd started the flight, Dani had looked so pale he worried she was going to pass out, but now she was pointing out buildings as they flew by, only occasionally gripping the edge of her seat when he changed direction. If he ever did do adventure tours, he knew he'd find a way to get her to go with him. Unlike Sophie, she'd break eventually. His ex had been all for him going out on his own, but the few times he said he'd wait for Dani to visit and go with him, he'd gotten a death glare and the silent treatment. And just when he thought she'd let it go, they'd have to "talk it out," which always ended in an argument. It only got worse over time. Whenever the phone rang, Sophie would be hovering, wanting to know who it was. And every time it was Dani, he'd wind up alone in his apartment instead of her staying the night.

A couple of weeks after Sophie had dumped him, when he felt like hell and missed her like crazy, he'd picked up the phone, planning on calling and telling her he'd do anything to fix them. Even cut Dani out of his life—after all, she'd picked Steve and moved with him to Little Rock, even after Wes told her he didn't want her to go.

"Did you and Steve fight a lot about us being so close?"

Dani slowly twisted to face him. "It came up a lot, yeah. It's one reason I couldn't come when you were celebrating getting your pilot's license. Now I hate that I let him stop me."

"You didn't miss much. Sophie threw the party, so it was all champagne and plates of hard-to-pronounce food." Dani would've made the party more fun, but her being there would've probably just caused a fight between him and Sophie, and that was back when he was still convinced they'd work everything out because they loved each other.

"I thought if I could show him I was devoted enough to move with him... But it seemed like we only argued more in Arkansas—about really stupid things, too, nothing and everything. He was stressed, I was stressed, and money started being an issue. And then he'd be, like, you don't talk to me, but you're on the phone all the time with Wes." She shook her head and leaned back in her seat. "I think he thought the friendship wouldn't last the move. Like I'd give you up that easily."

A solid rock of guilt formed in Wes's stomach. Now he felt even worse that he'd thought about cutting her out of his life. Even when he'd been considering it, though, he knew he'd never be able to go through with it. It wasn't easy to find a girl who made Indiana Jones references, had a killer fade-away shot, and was so easy to talk to. Hours trickled by whenever they spoke on the phone, even though it only seemed like minutes.

"I don't understand why people can't get over the fact that you and I actually are *just friends*," he said. "That we'll always be friends and nothing more. Is it really that hard to grasp?"

Dani glanced out her window. For a moment he thought

he'd said something wrong, but then she looked at him and shrugged. "I guess it is. Not sure if that makes us lucky or screwed up."

"Probably a little of both," he said, and she laughed.

Being here with her now, truly happy for the first time in months, he was sure he'd made the right decision. He needed Dani in his life, no matter what.

Wes focused his attention on landing as they neared the tour office. He held the helicopter steady and then slowly lowered it, kissing the landing skids on the ground and easing off the accelerator.

Dani released the grip she had on her seat.

"You okay?" he asked.

She nodded. "I expected a bumpier landing. I'd say something about your smoothness, but I'm sure I'd end up regretting it." Smiling, he took off his headphones and made sure everything was shut down.

His phone beeped. He pulled it out and stared at the screen, expecting another *Have you gotten your hair cut yet?* text from Audrey. But it wasn't his sister.

He looked at Dani. "When's the last time you played ball?"

She handed him her headphones. "I play the occasional pickup game at the gym. Why?"

"How'd you like to make an easy fifty bucks?"

Chapter Five

Dani kicked off her shoes by Wes's front door and then flopped onto his couch. Her muscles burned from what she'd just put them through. "FYI, that was not as easy as you made it sound."

Wes placed the plastic bag on top of his coffee table and sat next to her. "But we pulled it off."

Back in college, they used to go down to the basketball courts and hustle guys out of their money so they could eat something other than ramen. They'd simply go up to a couple of guys who were playing ball and challenge them to a game, winner gets twenty bucks. The guys would always look at Dani, laugh, and in most cases, say, "You're on." Then, between her speed and ability to sink three-pointers and Wes's height and competitive nature, they'd proceed to wipe the floor with them.

Of course, she wasn't practicing several hours every day anymore, so in today's game they'd barely scraped by. Apparently the betting rate for a game with cocky businessmen was fifty bucks.

"That half-court shot you made there at the end saved us." Wes mimicked shooting the ball and made a *whoosh* sound.

She sank back against the cushions. "I wasn't sure I was going to make it."

"Their faces were worth more than the money." Wes pulled the white-and-red boxes out of the bag. The scent of garlic sauce and fried chicken made her stomach growl.

In a lot of ways, it was like being transported back in time four years. Sitting on Wes's couch—though this couch was actually comfy and not made of scratchy fabric—celebrating winning a basketball game and eating take-out.

He picked up a remote and turned on his stereo. Kelly Clarkson filled the room.

Yep, just like college. When she'd first met him, she'd expected death metal or classic rock. But he mostly listened to pop music. He'd had a thing for Kelly Clarkson ever since the first *American Idol.*

He leaned back, half an eggroll sticking out of his mouth, and said, "She can sing *and* she's hot, so don't even go there."

"I wasn't going to say a thing." She grabbed her box of orange chicken and a pair of chopsticks and dug into her food. She twisted, tucking her feet under Wes's legs.

He jerked to the side. "Holy crap, your feet are freezing! I can feel them through my shorts."

"Which is why I need you to warm them up."

"I'll never understand how it can be ninety degrees and your feet are still cold."

She caught a piece of chicken between her chopsticks, ignoring the cold comment in hopes he wouldn't make her move her feet. "Time to work out the details of our relationship. Guess we're stuck with the story about you proposing on a hike, and then re-proposing at a concert, since that's not weird or anything. When do we say this all happened? The transition from friends to more."

"How about when I went to help you out after your knee surgery? That was the last time we were even in the same state."

"You were still with Sophie then, so that'd probably be bad."

"Right…I didn't think about the time line. It's not like my family would know whether or not you were visiting me or I was going out there, though."

"Especially if we say we wanted to keep it on the down low, afraid it might mess up our friendship."

"Good, good. That sounds believable." He took a drink of his Coke and rested the cup on his knee. "So if you and Steve broke up, like, what? Four months ago?"

"Close enough. It was two weeks before my surgery. Just long enough for him to move out and leave me without a ride. Until you showed up. Total Knight in Shining Armor move, by the way, so it's too bad we can't use that. When did you and Sophie break up exactly?"

"A couple of weeks after I got back from visiting you. Okay, so we'll say that I started calling you more and more, we kept talking…"

"I came to visit a couple of times." The lemonade she'd gotten must've been light, because it tasted like water with a disgusting lemony aftertaste. She reached across Wes, grabbed his Coke from his hand, and took a long pull, then gave it back. "And suddenly we realized that we were perfect for each other."

"Works for me," he said.

"So we'll say we were a couple for two months and then we decided to get engaged. Is that too fast?"

"In real life, maybe. I think it'll be fine for our fake engagement." He put his empty carton on the coffee table and sat back.

She caught a whiff of cologne, musky and woodsy, with a mixture of outdoors and even sweat. It shouldn't have smelled good to her, but it made a flutter go through her chest. Her gaze traveled up his muscled arms, well-built pecs, and settled on his face. She found herself thinking about all of his good qualities. How she'd never find a guy as good as him to date. How stupid Sophie was for dumping him.

I guess I'm stupid for not dating him myself.

Then she remembered how their one attempt to move the slightest bit past friends had not only crashed and burned but also nearly ruined their friendship.

He really is the whole package, though.

Wes's eyebrows drew together. "What? Why are you looking at me like that?"

She glanced away, heat rising in her cheeks. "Just thinking."

"About what?"

She met his eyes, telling herself it didn't mean anything that her stomach lurched. "Just about today. Being here with you. It's the most fun I've had in a long time."

He put his hand on her bare leg and squeezed. "Right back at you. And I'm glad your knee surgery hasn't slowed you down. When I first saw the cut, I thought you'd never be able to walk normally again, much less play ball."

All her blood seemed to rush to where his hand was warming her skin, and she suddenly had to work at getting words to come out of her mouth. "Well, if I hadn't had you there to help me recover, I probably would've pushed myself too hard and never fully healed."

Wes brushed his fingers across the scar on her knee, and her leg involuntarily twitched at his touch. She hoped he didn't notice.

She wished *she* didn't. But her heart was beating faster, and the way he was running his fingertips along her knee was sending little zips of heat across her skin.

Pull it together, Dani. He's your best friend. Don't screw it up now because you've gone without so much as a hug from a guy in months.

She swung her feet to the ground and stood so fast sparks of light danced across her vision. "I'm beat. I'm gonna go to bed."

"Okay. I'll be up for a little while, but I'll turn down the music."

"No worries. I sleep through anything, remember?" Most famously, she'd slept through a fire alarm. Luckily, Wes had been passed out on her couch and had to basically carry her out of her apartment.

She waved—cursing herself for the stupid, awkward gesture—and rushed back to the bedroom. Closing the door, she shook her head.

What the hell was that all about? Even though she knew she'd never be able to sleep, she crawled into bed. Wes's bed.

Earlier today, she'd been right there with him when he'd said they were friends and would never be more. So why was she noticing the way he smelled, and why was her skin humming under his touch? Why was she suddenly so aware of the fact that Wes usually slept where she was now?

I've got to stop thinking about all of his good qualities and remind myself why we're wrong for each other.

He was way too impulsive, which was great for a friend but not what she needed for a stable relationship. They lived completely different lives in completely different states. He'd made it clear he only thought of her as a friend. She was pretty sure he was still hung up on his ex.

And we don't have any romantic chemistry, anyway.

It was hard to tell herself that they had no chemistry when she could still feel the ghost of his touch on her knee. But he'd done more than touch her knee before, and it had been a disaster.

The air changed, heavy and pressing against her as she closed her eyes and relived a college memory—one she'd tried to pretend never happened.

Dani stumbled into Wes's apartment, tripping over the books and clothes piled on the floor. They'd won sixty bucks playing ball over the weekend and that night, they'd used the money on pizza and cheap beer. Lots and lots of beer. It was the first time she'd seen Wes so drunk he could hardly walk.

She fell onto the barely padded couch, closing her eyes to keep the room from spinning. The cushions sank with Wes's weight. "I still can't believe we pulled off that last game," he said, the words running together.

When Dani opened her eyes, his face was close to hers. So close, his features were blurred. Or maybe that was an effect of the alcohol. For some reason, she found this really funny and started giggling.

Then Wes was laughing, and she didn't think either of them had any idea why. Wes's hand landed high on her thigh, stifling the laughter. "You know, I partnered with you in class because I thought you were hot. I figured I was smart enough to float us, even if you were dumb."

She frowned, trying to decide if she'd just been insulted.

He placed his other hand on the side of her face. "But you're smart and *funny, and a hell of a ball player. Who knew it'd turn into this."*

This? *Her pulse skittered, and while everything had been blurry moments ago, things were sharpening at the corners now, along with the realization that his words and touch were sending butterflies through her stomach. What* was *this turning into? So far, it'd been a friendship so easy and fun, she'd actually turned down dates with perfectly good-looking guys to hang out with Wes. Yes, she'd sometimes wondered what would happen if they crossed into more, but now she wasn't sure it was a good idea.*

"Wes…?" The other words she meant to say caught in her throat. He was leaning closer.

Then his lips were on hers. She closed her eyes, waiting for her head to spin and for the desire to pull him closer.

But it wasn't there. In fact, she'd feel more of a spark if she licked an outlet. She pulled away, and he practically fell on top of her. Unsure what else to do, she pushed herself to her feet.

Wes held up his hands, like he was surrendering. "Shit, Dani. That wasn't… I didn't mean… I thought that maybe…" He shook his head. "That was awful, wasn't it?"

Okay, so she hadn't been into it, but "awful"? That was a little harsh. Maybe I suck at kissing. Maybe that's why I rarely go on second dates.

Chest aching, she said, "I gotta go."

Then she was out the door, occasionally holding onto the wall for support as she stumbled away from his apartment and into the cold night. As she walked home, tears slid down her cheeks. Because she knew no matter how good of friends they'd been, that kiss had ruined everything.

Dani opened her eyes, the memory of that first—and only—kiss with Wes burned into her mind. After that day, they didn't sit by each other in class, didn't hang out. Didn't do anything but run in the other direction when they saw each other. The distance between them had been painful, and she'd hurt every time she'd go to call him and realize she couldn't anymore.

Luckily, they'd finally talked about what had happened. Both of them agreed it was just a drunken mistake, so they would pretend it never happened and go back to being friends. She worried they wouldn't be able to, and the first few hangouts were pretty awkward. But gradually, things between them got back to normal. Back to being friends so close they could read each other's thoughts, back to counting on the other person to be there if they needed someone to talk to at three a.m., and back to spending more time together than apart.

That night all those years ago, they'd learned Friends With Benefits just wasn't for them. The benefit of their friendship was having someone to rely on without the drama that came along with kissing and dating and all those other complications.

Determined to squash any attraction her stupid body was telling her she felt, she rolled over in the bed. She caught a whiff of the same amazing musky scent she'd smelled earlier, though...

And she couldn't help but wonder if Wes had gotten better at kissing over the years.

Chapter Six

Dani had hoped she'd feel better after a good night's sleep. Maybe it was because she'd tossed and turned instead, but her emotions were still a big confusing mess. She was almost scared to go out and see Wes, for fear she hadn't sufficiently snuffed out her sudden attraction to him.

The knock on the bedroom door made her jump. "Just gotta grab my clothes," Wes said.

Dani ran a hand down her hair. "Come on in."

He strolled in wearing a towel around his waist, his hair damp and extra wavy, and her heart immediately picked up speed. Nope, the attraction wasn't gone.

Focus on the awful kiss. But that didn't work, because then she was looking at his lips.

He pulled some jeans off a hanger, looping them over his arm, and then reached inside the closet again. "I don't remember buying this." He lifted the purple dress she'd brought to wear to the wedding.

"I hung it up so it wouldn't get wrinkled," Dani said.

Two creases formed between his eyebrows, getting

deeper as he twisted it one way and then the other. "Why's the zipper in the front? It looks backwards."

"That's because that's not the front." She'd bought the low-back dress shortly after Steve had dumped her and she wanted to feel sexy and bold, which was also how she'd felt when she packed it. Now she was worried it was a mistake. Especially with Wes's insightful fashion commentary.

"Maybe you've been wearing it wrong."

Dani swiped it out of his hand and hung it back up. "I'm not taking fashion tips from someone wearing a towel."

"It's distracting, isn't it," he said with a grin.

She rolled her eyes, but inside she was screaming, *yes, yes it is*. Especially since there was still a sheen of water from his shower across his skin, there was something intriguing about the way the tattoo highlighted his muscles, and the masculine soap scent was filling the air, making her want to lean in and take a deep breath of it.

When he'd been ranting yesterday about people not understanding how they could only be friends, he'd made it clear that was all he'd ever feel for her. It made her bounce between scolding herself for caring and wondering why she did.

She grabbed her clothes and left him to change. As she showered and got ready for the day, she still felt like her mood was on an up-and-down roller coaster. It was a relief when Wes finally pulled up to his parents' house, simply because it'd give her a distraction from staring at him and feeling that traitorous squeeze of her heart.

Dani put her hand on his arm, then pulled it back when she noticed how firm it felt. And then she was thinking once again about how good he looked in only a towel. "Um, we never discussed a date or a location for the wedding or colors or any of that."

"Ever since I found out the museum held weddings,

I thought it would be cool to get married there," Wes said. "That way if I got bored, I could wander out to the exhibits in my tux."

"Glad you think our wedding is going to be so boring," she said, mocking offense. "Okay, so the museum. I'm sure the waiting list is long, so we'll say we're working on a date, but it'll probably be about a year. Do we want to pick a color theme? Your mom and sisters were talking about that the other night, too."

"Just not canary."

She guessed from his tone that canary must've been Sophie's pick. "Flamingo it is, then," she joked, and one corner of his mouth kicked up. "How 'bout we stick with blue for our college color?"

"Works for me."

"Do you think your mom and sisters would have a heart attack if I said I also wanted bulldog centerpieces? After all, I was a Bulldog for four years. Don't want to let my alma mater down."

That glow he got when he was about to pull off a prank or a stunt hit his eyes. "Five bucks if you tell them that. But you gotta do it totally straight-faced."

Man, she wanted to take that challenge. "Maybe we shouldn't give half of your family heart attacks before your sister's wedding. Especially since I'm not sure Audrey likes me so much."

"She's not mad at you; she's mad at me. I'm telling you, everything offends her lately. I mean, can you believe she wants me to get rid of this?" He ran a hand across his whiskered jaw. "Like it's not refined enough for a wedding."

"Sorry, but I'm with her on that. I'm all for a five o'clock shadow, but you're pushing more like nine or ten o'clock and it's starting to look more mountain man than groomsman."

He shook his head. "Man, no love for the beard." They

got out of the car and started up the sidewalk.

"I guess we should…" He grabbed her hand, opened the door, and led them inside. "Anybody home? I was told there was some kind of party to set up for."

Kathleen came out of the kitchen and smiled at her son. "Just in time." Her warm eyes moved to Dani. "So nice to see you again, Danielle."

"She goes by Dani, actually," Wes said.

"I was only ever called Danielle when I was in trouble, and it came along with all of my names in rapid succession, all Danielle Caridad Morales Vega! Followed by a stream of Spanish swear words, usually." She clamped her lips, wondering why she'd just shared way too much information, but Kathleen's smile only widened.

"Caridad Morales Vega," Wes repeated as though he were committing it to memory. "What do they mean in English?"

Dani glanced at his mom and then back at him. "Caridad means charity and Morales is my mom's maiden name. That's how it works in Mexico."

"Charity," Wes said. "That fits."

She thought he was teasing her, but when she met his eyes, he seemed genuine. A surge of affection for him went through her, and she gave his hand a squeeze. Time slowed down for a moment, and she was back to thinking of how funny and smart and sexy he was. Then she remembered his mom was standing right there.

Dani smiled at Kathleen, wanting Wes's mom to like her, regardless of the fact that she wouldn't actually be marrying her son. "So what do you need help with?"

"Centerpieces," Kathleen said. "I could use a female opinion, and Audrey's not here yet. And Wes, your father's out back, hitching the trailer to the truck. He's about to go pick up all the tables and chairs. Apparently the last people who used them set them up by the lake and it was all rainy, so they're covered with mud. We're going to have to clean each chair." She ran a hand through her gray-blond bob. "So much to do. I'm not sure how we're going to pull off this wedding tomorrow."

"We'll make it work, Ma. Don't worry." Wes put his hands on the sides of Dani's waist and leaned in close, his warm breath hitting her neck. "Will you be okay here for a little while without me?"

Where was all the air, because it felt like it'd been sucked out of the room. Her heart was beating too fast and too loud, and she was terrified Wes would notice and ask what her deal was. And since she didn't know herself, she had no idea what she'd say. She managed to nod and pull off a breathy, "Yeah."

His lips brushed her ear and heat pooled low in her stomach. "If you get nervous, just start going through history facts in your head. That seemed to work pretty well yesterday." He pulled back and shot her a smile, and then went out the back door.

When Dani glanced back toward Kathleen, she was grinning from ear to ear.

"He's so much happier around you. I was worried about him for a while, and now… Well, now it looks like I don't have to worry." Kathleen beckoned her inside the kitchen. There were flowers and vases and candles covering every surface— it looked like a craft store had exploded.

She picked up a bag with multicolored rocks that rattled together when she lifted it. "I thought we had everything under control, but now I'm wondering what we were thinking not hiring a wedding planner. I mean, I know we were thinking we couldn't afford one and how hard could it be to throw a wedding, right? Do you think it's too late?"

Dani stared at Kathleen, not sure what to say.

Kathleen grabbed her hand and patted it. "That was a

joke. The rest of our help will arrive soon, and it'll all come together. It's going to look worse before it gets better—just remember that as you're pulling together *your* wedding." She kept talking, moving to grab boxes.

All Dani could think was, weird feelings for her best friend aside, she was *so* not ready to plan or put on a wedding.

· · ·

The first thing Wes noticed when Dad pulled up to the house was Sophie's Audi sitting in the driveway. The Audi he'd gone with her to buy. He'd gotten distracted looking at the sports cars and big trucks at the dealership next door, but she'd had her heart set on that model and actually got upset he wasn't more enthusiastic about it and all its special features.

He usually felt exhausted when he saw her car and realized that he'd have to be around her. Conversations were strained and a lot of work, and his family always looked at him like he was going to fall apart, when really he just didn't want to go through the motions of pretending they'd be friends someday.

But it'd be different now, because he'd have Dani to help him forget about all the drama.

After months of feeling like he was the underdog in this situation, showing his ex he was fine without her was going to be a welcome change. He walked around the house to the back, where his relatives were in wedding prep mode. He scanned the faces, looking for Dani, hoping the wedding and his family hadn't overwhelmed her yet. They still had two heavily scheduled days ahead of them.

He found Sophie first. Her pale blond hair was pulled up, her cheeks were pink from the sun, and even though they'd be setting up for the wedding all day, she had on a lacy white top and jeans with rhinestones on the pockets. She glanced up at him and gave him a forced smile and a tiny wave. He nodded. See? Awkward.

The sound of the sliding patio door caught his attention. Dani stepped out, her dark hair piled in a messy bun on top of her head. Knowing her, she was probably regretting not bringing her baseball hat to block the sun. "While you were on your getting-chairs adventure, I learned how to make centerpieces. It was…fun."

"And did you bring up the fact that you want bulldog centerpieces at our wedding?"

She wrinkled her nose. "Our wedding. That still sounds so weird."

"You're avoiding the question."

She bit her lip.

"Guess you owe me five bucks."

"I almost brought it up twice," Dani said, "but your mom's so nice, and after the lengthy sermon on floral arrangements, I just couldn't bring up bulldogs."

"Chicken."

She shoved him. "I think I'm still ahead. Just take it out of the ten dollars you owe me. Besides, the day's not over yet."

Out of the corner of his eye, he noticed Sophie staring. He grabbed Dani's hand, pulled her next to him, and swept her hair out of her face. "We've got an audience, so I figure we might as well play this up."

He expected a smile, but when her eyes met his, she looked a little sad.

"What? Is something wrong?"

"Nope. Everything's great," she said, too quickly. Then she reached up and tugged on a piece of his hair. Her hand dropped down to his shoulder and ran along his arm.

"Ew, are you guys going to kiss?"

Wes's six-year-old nephew stared up at them, his lower lip

jutting out and his nose wrinkled in disgust.

"Mason. Let's leave Uncle Wes alone." Jill smiled at them. Then she stuck a hand on her hip and tilted her head. Uh-oh. "You know, I've never seen any engaged couple who's not permanently attached at the mouth. Just look at Audrey and Matthew. They kiss between every word they speak. I can hardly be around them."

She gestured to the couple, and sure enough, they were kissing.

It seemed easy enough to play off his and Dani's engagement with the ring and the formal announcement. He hadn't thought about the kissing part. He wondered if everyone had noticed. If Sophie had noticed.

He glanced down at Dani. Time to take this act to the next level.

• • •

After an entire day of not being able to stop looking at Wes, Dani purposely kept her gaze away from him. Especially now that his sister was talking about kissing. She fiddled with her belt loop. "Yeah, we're not really big on PD—"

Wes jerked her to him and smashed his lips onto hers. His scratchy whiskers scraped against her skin, and her back cracked as he dramatically dipped her. Then she was yanked upright just as roughly. She clung to him, trying to recover from the whiplash kissing. A laugh was bubbling up, but she clenched her jaw, not wanting to blow their cover. She widened her eyes at him, silently asking what the hell that was about, and he winked at her. Obviously he was just hamming it up, playing his part.

And while the rational part of her brain knew it wasn't a real kiss, and of course he wouldn't want to actually kiss her, since he made it clear they were *only friends*, she couldn't help but feel a pinch of disappointment. So many of her guy problems could be solved if she started a relationship with the one she'd most like to spend all her time with.

"That's so gross," Mason said, his lip curling. "You're going to have girl cooties."

Wes's arm tightened around her. "You'll understand someday, little man."

Jill shook her head, but she was staring at Wes and Dani like they were adorable. "I'm going to see if Mom needs more help with the centerpieces."

"Wes and I are having bulldog centerpieces at our wedding," Dani blurted out.

Jill's mouth opened, closed. Then she just turned around and went into the house.

"You owe me five dollars," Dani said to Wes. She ran a hand across her skin, where she could still feel the aftereffects of his whiskers against her mouth. "Your beard is seriously so scratchy."

He burrowed his head in her neck, rubbing his stubble there.

She tried to shove him away, but he wrapped his arms tighter around her and moved the assault to her shoulder. She laughed, trying to get a hand between his face and her skin. "Okay, that's enough. I'm going to look like I made out with a porcupine."

A prickling went across her skin, not from the whiskers but from behind her. She glanced over her shoulder and felt the full impact of Sophie's stare. It was heavy and laser-beam-like, with lots of bitterness and loathing thrown in.

Wes grabbed her hand, apparently not noticing the dirty looks. "Come help me unload the chairs. We'll clean off the mud and you won't have to hear talk of centerpieces *or* flowers."

On the way to the truck, she noticed Audrey was also

glaring at them, lips pursed.

Looks like we'll have pissed off the entire wedding party by the end of the day. Dani didn't want to care, but why couldn't Audrey accept their engagement? Did she think that Sophie was a better choice?

The thought sent a twisting, burning sensation through her gut. She didn't want to analyze what that meant. She needed to just relax and enjoy being around Wes without making a complicated mess out of everything.Wes and his dad unloaded the tables and chairs, and Dani got to work cleaning them off with a soapy bucket of water and a sponge. Every time Wes passed, he would brush his face across her bare skin. He even placed a few scratchy kisses on her cheek.

The next time he came around, she lifted her dripping sponge. "Stay back."

"Or what?"

"Don't you see I'm armed?"

"A sponge? You're going to have to do better than that."

She tossed it at him, but he dodged it and came at her. She picked up the bucket of soapy water and launched it at him. The stream hit him right in the face, a full blast she hadn't expected to land.

For a moment, he stared, water dripping from his hair.

Then he lunged, wrapping his arms around her waist. They fell to the ground, sliding on the wet grass. Wes straddled her and rubbed his wet hair in her face.

"Stop! Stop it!" she squealed, but she was laughing too hard for the words to have much power.

"Wes!" yelled a much angrier voice. Audrey stood above them, arms crossed. Wes glanced up, and Dani could see the wheels turning, some kind of smartass remark forming on his tongue.

"You might want to reconsider whatever you're planning on saying," Dani whispered. "She looks pretty pissed."

Wes pushed himself up and helped her to her feet. His gaze dropped to her chest, and she realized that the neckline of her shirt had shifted, revealing quite a bit of her red bra. He quickly looked away, a guilty expression on his face.

Well, at least I know the reason we don't have chemistry isn't because he thinks I'm hideous, she thought as she readjusted her clothes.

"Can I talk to you?" Audrey's eyes flicked to Dani, then back to Wes. "Alone."

"Hint taken." Dani backed away. She widened her eyes, flashing Wes the same look she gave him when they used to get busted in class for talking, and she could see he was trying not to laugh. Then she spun around to leave them alone.

And came face to face with Sophie.

Chapter Seven

"What are you thinking?" Audrey's nostrils flared, something Wes wanted to tease her about, but decided he'd better not—she was already angry enough. It wasn't easy not to laugh, though, especially since Dani had been shooting him a face that said, *You're so screwed, sucker.*

"Come on. Did getting engaged ruin your sense of humor?"

"It certainly hasn't ruined yours. In fact, I'd like you to take it down about a hundred notches." Audrey pinched the bridge of her nose. "What are you thinking, Wes? You show up the other night, tell us you're engaged, and now you're all over Dani every second with no care for what it's doing to everyone else?"

He folded his arms and leaned his hip against one of the dining room chairs. "Everyone else? Who am I hurting?"

Audrey tilted her head. "Like you don't know."

"What I know is you kept telling me I should move on. I thought this was what you, Jill, and Mom wanted. Hell, even Sophie apparently wants it. That's the message I got."

"Sure. We wanted you to move on. Not go and get engaged days before my wedding. Do you know what this means?"

"That I'm happy." As he said the words, he realized it was true. He'd spent hours in the same vicinity as Sophie, and he was still happy. In fact, he'd forgotten she was even there.

Audrey gave an exasperated sigh. "It means more drama between you and Sophie."

"Hey, you're the one who invited her to be part of your wed—"

"This isn't about you!" Audrey's voice pitched up, the way it did when she was angry or about to cry; Wes wasn't sure which one right now. The wedding mess had seemed to cause tension between him and his sister lately, and it sucked. It was like he was always walking on eggshells, and he missed how things used to be. He and Audrey had always been close, always teasing each other and joking around. Of course they'd fought plenty growing up. But they had each other's backs when it came down to it, and seeing her upset was a punch to his gut.

She shook her head. "That's what you've never gotten. You can't just let me have a moment in the spotlight, can you? Now everyone's buzzing about you and Dani and the fact that you're engaged now and… Ugh!" A deep crease formed between her eyebrows.

He hadn't thought of how his fake announcement and fake fiancée would affect his sister's big day. She'd definitely be even angrier if he admitted it was all a big sham. Maybe he hadn't been as supportive through all the wedding stress as he should've been, he realized, and he decided that he'd do better, even if he didn't understand why things like flowers and decorations were such a big deal.

"Tell you what. To make up for my stealing your thunder, I'll try to hold back the fart jokes at your wedding. I'm classy like that."

The corners of her mouth quivered, but she lost the fight and broke into a smile. She shoved him, and the chair he was leaning against knocked into the table. "I hate you," she said.

"You're crazy about me. I'm your favorite brother."

She sighed, and the last of her anger faded. "I know you didn't do this on purpose, because you never think things through. And I *am* happy you've moved on. I'd freak out over how fast it was if it were anyone but Dani, but you two have been dancing around this for years anyway." She lifted her eyes to his. "But can't you guys tone it down a bit? It's like you're rubbing Sophie's face in your new love, and she's all broken up about it."

He almost denied the "dancing around this for years" comment out of habit, but it *was* what had helped sell the engagement ruse so easily. And lately he'd felt like they *were* doing some kind of dance—one he didn't know the steps to. He pushed those thoughts away and focused on the Sophie issue. "I don't know why she'd care." Especially since she was the one who showed up with a guy shortly after their breakup, rubbing how little she cared in his face.

Audrey tilted her head. "Of course she cares. You two might've broken up, but I don't think she quite got over you, either. I thought that maybe you two might eventually work it out, but now... Well, now you're with Dani, and that's fine, but just think how you'd feel if it were Sophie doing all the kissing with another guy."

Wes waited for that image to bother him, but it didn't. He didn't exactly want to see it, but he could handle it. His thoughts bounced back to Dani and how she shrieked every time he rubbed his whiskers against her bare skin. Then his mind replayed the image of her red bra. He'd tried not to stare, but it was hard not to. He wasn't immune to breasts just because she was his best friend.

When he looked up, Audrey's eyebrows were raised, like

she was waiting for something. "I get it. Less kissing Dani."

"And less making a mess of my wedding decorations with your water fights." She eyed him.

"You got it. But remember to have some fun, too. This is supposed to be a celebration, not a cause for an aneurism." He nudged her. "A little fun goes a long way to relieve some stress. Or you could go all out and do something really fun so you and Matthew don't turn into a boring married couple."

"You don't think he's bored, do you?" Audrey asked.

Wes bit back a laugh, afraid she'd take it as him thinking it was the case, when really he knew it wasn't true at all. "He's crazy about you. It's kind of disgusting, actually."

She grinned.

"You know you can still call me, whenever, for whatever. And if you need to get away for a bit, I happen to have a helicopter at my disposal."

"Thanks, Wes." She gave him a quick hug before going back outside.

Well, that conversation went much better than he'd expected, especially after how rough it started out. Kind of funny he was getting scolded for kissing Dani when he *hadn't* kissed her—not really. Wanting to avoid any weirdness after, he'd given her more of a lip-smashing assault, all for show. He hadn't wondered in years what it would be like to *really* kiss her. Not since that drunken night in college. All he remembered was her leaving and all of the awkwardness that came after.

"Pull it together," he muttered to himself, shaking his head. No kissing her. Not for real.

No matter what.

. . .

"I knew it." Sophie's lips twisted as she looked Dani up and down. It was the way Wes's girlfriend—ex-girlfriend now, thank goodness—always used to look at her, even when she was pretending to be nice.

Dani froze in place, wanting to flee, yet needing to stand firm, no matter what insults this girl was about to hurl at her. But then she saw something on her face that wasn't normally there—a hint of sorrow just underneath the irritation.

"He denied it so many times, but I knew he was in love with you." Sophie sniffed and—oh, hell—tears were gathering in her eyes.

Dani wasn't sure if talking to her would make it better or worse, but she figured the girl should at least know she hadn't been cheated on. "He wasn't in love with me when he was dating you, Sophie. We were living in different states and never even saw each other." *And you were taking up* all *of his time.*

Sophie shook her head so violently some of her hair came out of her updo. "You don't have to keep denying it. When he went to Arkansas to take care of you after your surgery instead of coming to my parents' with me for their anniversary party, I knew he'd always choose you."

Dani didn't realize Wes had canceled plans in order to help her recover from her knee surgery. All she knew was he'd shown up just when she needed him and stayed with her until she was back on her feet—or foot, as it were. She'd used crutches for a while.

"That wasn't because he was in love with me," Dani said. "I told him I'd be fine, but he knew my mom couldn't come and that I didn't have anyone else to help me out. If he hadn't done it, I honestly don't know how I would've survived those awful days after, when I couldn't even move."

"Well, it doesn't really matter *when* he fell in love with you, does it? You always came first, and now he's yours." Her gaze moved to the diamond ring on Dani's finger. "Actually,

I'm glad this happened. Now I don't feel so stupid for dumping him. I knew I was right, but it's nice to really *know*, instead of having to question over and over if I made the right decision."

You still love him, Dani thought, but she didn't dare say it out loud, not sure what it would mean for her or Sophie. Or Wes.

Sophie sniffed again, then turned away and strode to the house, no doubt going inside to have herself a cry.

Dani's mind whirred over everything she'd just discovered. She *had* told Wes he didn't need to come help her after her knee surgery, even though she'd known she was going to be screwed with no help. When he'd shown up in time to take her to the hospital, she'd almost turned into a crying mess. The selfish part of her was glad to know he'd blown off Sophie and her family to be there, because she did always want to come first in his life.

But now that she knew he and Sophie still had feelings for each other, and that her being there was only making their reconciliation more unlikely, she felt like she should back down.

A hand on her shoulder made her turn. "So Audrey thinks we're rubbing our love into Sophie's face too much." Wes grinned. "Guess we're better actors than I thought."

"Sounds like we've got everybody fooled." Here was the part where she should tell him to go get the girl he was actually in love with and forget about this ruse.

But a small voice whispered, *He's* supposed *to be mine.*

Her phone rang, and she slid it out of her pocket. Yes, she was stalling, but when she saw it was the office, she was glad she hadn't ignored it. She held up a finger and took a couple of steps away from Wes.

"Mr. Halifax just said he wasn't sure our marketing plan was the best for his company. This is why I told you that you needed to be here for this!" Bill was the pompous jerk with the fancy-pants marketing degree who had gotten promoted over her two years ago. Unfortunately, her junior exec status meant she had to take too much of his crap.

She worked to keep calm. "I already took care of everything. All you had to do was present it to him. It should've been an easy sell."

"Well if that were the case, he would've signed the contract, wouldn't he?"

Frustration was rising through her, bringing her blood pressure up with it. She rubbed her forehead, trying to figure out the solution. "I'll call him. I'll fix it. I've just got to get back to my computer to access the presentation. I'll call you back when I'm done talking to him."

"You know Wayne will have both our jobs if this deal falls through."

She bit back her *Yeah, asshole, I know* comment and hung up. She turned to Wes. "Work emergency. I've gotta get back to the apartment."

Wes dug into his pocket and took out his keys. "Take my car. I'll get a ride home from someone."

Out of the corner of her eye, she saw Sophie watching them. And she thought, whether or not Sophie and Wes eventually got back together, the girl should at least have to suffer a little longer by seeing what she missed out on. So she stepped forward and kissed Wes's cheek. "Thanks."

Dani stared at her phone, finger hovering over the last digit she needed to push. She'd fought hard to be able to work on Mr. Halifax's account, and if it fell through, she could forget about a promotion, no matter what happened at the company retreat.

But if I pull this off... She was always looked down on

because she had a degree in history instead of marketing—like that really mattered. She'd had a crash course in real-world marketing, starting out as an assistant and clawing her way up to junior account executive. And though it might sound cocky, she was smarter than half the people at that office, and her social skills were definitely better.

I can do this. I can do this.

She made the call, her heart in her throat.

Spending an hour on the phone with their client was slightly torturous, but she managed to remind Mr. Halifax of all the reasons why she was right about his marketing campaign. By the end of the call, she'd convinced him to sign the contract and fax it to the office.

"From now on, I'm dealing solely with you," Mr. Halifax said. "I don't want to bother anymore with that idiot I talked to earlier today."

Dani smiled. Hearing Bill called an idiot was worth the long phone call and going over every detail twenty times. *Which just proves a degree in marketing or the fact he's now married doesn't make him any better at this job than I am.* But as much as she would love to bash him, it was important to remain professional. "I took point on this account, and again, I'm sorry I wasn't there to clarify everything. My fiancé's sister is getting married, and I'm down in North Carolina for the wedding."

The lie was getting easier to tell now, though the guilt was still there, hanging heavy in her stomach.

"Well, family is important. You have fun, and tell that fiancé of yours he's marrying one smart cookie." After she hung up, she called Bill to tell him the news, trying to keep the smugness out of her voice. Of course he'd probably take credit, especially with her out of the office. All her life, she'd asked Mama to relax and not take work so seriously. Now here she was, worrying she shouldn't have taken time off, understanding the pressure her mom had been under all those years. As she thought over the last few days, though, she wouldn't trade them for the world.

Days she hadn't had to think about everything that'd been stressing her out for months.

I should call and check in. The last thing she wanted was to get on the phone again, but she still dialed her mom. The second Mama answered, she could hear the exhaustion in her voice.

"I hadn't called in a while and thought I'd say hello. How's Abuela doing today?"

"Oh, feisty as ever. Her spirit's there. If only her body… She thinks she can still do everything, but I see her clutching her chest. We fought over the oxygen like we do every day, and finally I got her to sit down and breathe with it on for a while. The doctor wants to put her on a new medication."

New medication probably meant more money. Talking about it would only stress out Mama more, though, so Dani asked, "How are *you* doing?"

Mama never complained about herself. She said she was hanging in there, talked a little bit about work, and asked how she was. Dani probably should've mentioned she was visiting Wes, but Mama would want to know what was going on, and she had this way of prying information out of her. Not to mention the fact that Mama always asked about Wes in that way that made it clear she wouldn't mind having him for a son-in-law. So they made a few more minutes of small talk and then said their good-byes and I-love-yous.

Stifling a yawn, Dani grabbed the bag of potato chips Wes had left on the coffee table and dug in. She punched on the television and sank onto the couch. After a little while, she closed her eyes, thinking she'd just take a rest, so she'd be up for some more fun with Wes when he got home.

It was good to have time to think over everything

rationally. They were friends who had a blast together, their relationship blissfully uncomplicated. If there were anything more between them, she would've at least felt a little something with that kiss today. In fact, her sudden attraction to him seemed silly now. And with it under control, she could just relax and enjoy hanging with her best friend.

She didn't want to think about the fact that a good best friend would tell Wes that the girl he was still in love with loved him back.

• • •

Wes opened the door to his apartment, eager to kick back with Dani, maybe watch a movie or play some video games. She was on the couch, curled into a ball. Her laptop was open on the coffee table, but the screen was black, so he assumed it'd been a while since she'd typed anything.

"Dani?"

She didn't lift her head. He tossed his keys off to the side. So much for asking her about his haircut. He was sure he hadn't gone as short as Audrey would've preferred, but he'd lost several inches. Without his face shaved, he looked especially odd, like his face and hair no longer matched.

I can't believe she can fall asleep like that. She's going to have a killer kink in her neck and back if she stays like this all night.

He decided he'd better move her to the bed. It seemed kind of weird to pick her up, but he knew better than to try to wake her. Not only would she sleep through it, she often swung her arms and kicked when anyone tried to interrupt her sleep. She claimed she had no memory of it the next morning, but he wondered if it weren't just a good excuse to beat up on him a bit without consequences.

Wes moved the bag of potato chips next to Dani off to

the side and scooped her up. A tiny moan escaped her lips and his throat went dry. He readjusted his hold on her. She felt smaller than he expected in his arms, her skin was so soft, and she wasn't kidding about having stuff to make her smell girlie. He wasn't sure if it were her shampoo or her perfume, but he wanted to bury his head in her neck and take in the subtle sweet scent. He laid her in his bed and she immediately rolled onto her side, tucking a hand under her face.

Wes sat down on the edge of the mattress. She looked so peaceful. Not that she usually didn't, but she'd always struck him as someone who could hold her own. Whereas his sisters and Sophie cried often, he'd only seen Dani kind of cry once. He'd heard the hint of it in her voice when she'd told Wes that Steve had dumped her, but there was no flood of tears or sobs.

But when it came down to helping people, she was the first to volunteer. And if someone was hurting, she knew just what to say to make him or her feel better. He realized he was already sad about her having to go back home, his chest aching at the thought, even though they still had a full day together tomorrow. They wouldn't really have the day, though, he thought. It would be filled with wedding stuff.

He ran his gaze up the length of her. He'd always known she was beautiful, but it struck him now stronger than ever, even stronger than the night he'd kissed her back in college. It was why he'd kissed her. But it had nearly ruined their friendship.

That was why he definitely shouldn't be thinking about running his fingers along her curves now. His breath grew shallow.

You just haven't been with anyone in a long time. She's here and she's fun and amazing.

And sexy.

He pushed himself off the bed, needing to put distance

between them before he did something stupid. As he left the room, he cast one last glance over his shoulder at her.

In his bed.

He gulped. He could feel the pulse at the base of his neck steadily picking up speed.

Don't even think about it. She's not *an option.*

So he took one more moment to acknowledge that, yes, she was sexy, and there was something inside of him whispering that maybe things would be different if he *really* kissed her. But she was his best friend, and even if she didn't freak out about him wanting more, they lived in different places. Lived different lives.

Lives that didn't involve him curling up next to her in bed and kissing every inch of her like he wanted to.

Chapter Eight

Dani woke up disoriented. She blinked against the bright stripe of sunlight coming through the window, then glanced at the alarm clock on the side table. When had night come and gone, and why didn't she remember any of it?

Fuzzy details from yesterday slowly came back to her. Helping set up for the wedding and messing around with Wes until they got in trouble. The work call with Mr. Halifax. Lying down on Wes's couch... And that was it. She must've fallen asleep. Which sucked. She hadn't wanted to waste the little bit of time she had left with Wes by sleeping.

How did she get here, though?

She vaguely recalled the sensation of being carried. *Wes must've brought me in here.* She wondered why he hadn't just left her on the couch and taken the bed. She kicked off the covers and got up. As she padded down the hall, she pulled her tangled hair into a ponytail. "Wes?"

He wasn't on the couch. She noticed a sheet of paper and keys on the coffee table.

Had to help out with some last-minute wedding stuff and didn't want to wake you. Left you my car so you can take your time. Go ahead and enjoy your morning off, hang in the city or whatever, and then you can meet me at the house later.

Wes

She wondered why he wouldn't want her help with the wedding errands. Maybe he needed space. Normally, she could understand that—she certainly smothered easily, though not when it came to spending time with Wes.

What if he finds out Sophie still loves him while they're getting ready for the wedding? Even though she'd planned on telling him, the thought of them together made her stomach knot. She had to remind herself again that she didn't want Wes, not like that.

Right?

But now she was remembering things she hadn't taken into account yesterday when she'd been drifting off to sleep. Like how, yes, his whiskers were scratchy, but there had been a tiny thrill that shot through her every time he'd brushed them against her skin. And the way he'd looked at her after the water fight…

That's just because he's a guy and I had a whole lot of cleavage on display. Of course, that hadn't stopped her heart from skipping a couple of beats. It was doing it now, too. She put her hand over her chest, as if that would stop it.

Crap. I thought I'd gotten rid of this odd crush-thing yesterday. Why wasn't her brain listening to all the reasons she and Wes were better off as friends and nothing more?

She sighed. It was going to be a long day, especially with all the extra craziness and emotions of the wedding. So maybe she would take the morning to go to her favorite places in Charlotte—who knew when she'd get another chance.

Another depressing thought.

For months she'd told herself Arkansas was her home now. It was where she worked. Where her apartment and all her earthly possessions were. But it was funny how Wes's place suddenly felt more like home than her own place did. Even though his cleaning had slipped over the last few days and it looked more like she'd first expected it to, with clothes hanging on the furniture and empty Coke cans left all around. Or maybe it wasn't so much his place as it was him.

Her chest tightened. *I have a feeling it's going to be hard to go back to my normal life after this.*

· · ·

Wes sat across from Mom, eating the breakfast she'd whipped up and sipping coffee.

"You look so handsome," Mom said, pushing the plate of bacon toward him. "What did Dani say about the new look? She like it?"

Wes ran his hand across his smooth cheek. After a couple months of not shaving, his face felt naked and exposed. "She hasn't seen it yet."

Confusion flickered across Mom's features.

"She was asleep when I got in last night," he said. "Think she had some work emergency and with all the traveling and everything…"

"Well, she's a dear girl. I see why you like her so much."

Yeah, he saw why he liked her so much, too. Now he needed to stop. It was like last night he'd gotten this idea that he and Dani were perfect for each other, and he couldn't shake it, no matter how much he told himself it would never end well. They worked because they didn't have drama or all the fights that came with romantic relationships. Everything he kept telling himself didn't stop this nagging *What if it worked* thought from coming up again and again, though.

Kissing her in college had been a disaster—or the aftereffects had been, anyway. Honestly, he only remembered snippets from that night. He'd been drunk and thinking she was hot and he'd decided to try it just once. Then she left and things were weird and he felt like an idiot for weeks afterward.

"Wes?"

He looked up from his food. "She's amazing."

"So when is she moving here?" Mom frowned. "You're not leaving, are you? You just got all settled into your new job, and I don't want you living so far away."

"Not sure." Wes stood to refill his coffee. "We haven't really talked about it."

"Haven't talked about it? Wes, those are things you need to discuss right away. Dani said you were getting married at the museum, so I thought that meant she wanted to be here in North Carolina. What was it she said she did? Something in marketing?"

Mom was reminding him of all the reasons he couldn't cross the line. Because if he did and she left for Arkansas, she might never come back. The awkwardness would stretch across several states, and without face-to-face time together, he'd lose her for good. That thought made his insides turn cold and hard.

He gave Mom a side-hug. "Let's just worry about one wedding at a time, okay?"

. . .

Dani turned onto the busy downtown streets, squinting at the road signs. She hadn't been here in years, and Wes had been doing the driving back then.

She needed to go somewhere to think but still have something else to focus on if her thoughts got too overwhelming. Even now, she was noticing how Wes's car smelled like him, and then she was thinking about his clear blue eyes and the image of him in a towel, all those muscles on display. This couldn't be healthy.

The street came up sooner than expected and she made a quick turn that made the tires squeal. Wes would've been proud—if it weren't his car.

She pulled into the parking garage of the place where she and Wes were supposed to get married. In theory, obviously. After all the craziness of yesterday, she was starting to think eloping was the way to go. No bird-named colors or centerpieces that took hours to arrange and place just so.

Of course, there was a chance her fiancé was currently in the process of getting back together with his ex-fiancée, which could really put a damper on wedding plans, big ceremony or Vegas chapel. How was she ever going to be okay with that? What if Wes and Sophie got re-engaged? Could she really go to their wedding and not stand up and object? Her insides clenched more with each thought, until tension stretched tight across her neck and shoulders.

She shoved out of the car and walked toward the museum's entrance, telling herself she could do it if being married to Sophie made Wes happy.

Yes, she could do it, but it would break her heart, knowing he was legally someone else's, till death do they part.

Dani blinked. She would not cry over a hypothetical situation—that was just stupid.

The scent of old meeting new filled the air of the museum: part cleaner, part items from long before she was born. Her muscles relaxed and everything inside her calmed. No more stressing over what was or wasn't happening with Wes. This time was about her. Who she was. Who she wanted to be. What she wanted.

She paid and then wandered from exhibit to exhibit,

taking her time to peruse the plaques, even the ones she'd read years before. Steve wasn't one for museums—his eyes went blank whenever she started going on about what she thought were perfectly interesting historical facts. Her passion had always been early America and post–Civil War America. The country had gone through so many changes in such a short amount of time.

And freedom was at the heart of it all. Her skin tingled with that thought. It was what good stories were based on, and it'd happened right here in her home country, hundreds of years ago.

Even though she was trying to be all "I'm discovering myself and fine on my own," she missed having Wes along. He never rushed her, and they could talk on and on about history, mixing speculation with fact and occasionally debating minor discrepancies.

She walked down the recreated main street with the African American barbershop and stopped in front of the Good Samaritan Hospital Chapel, one of the first African-American hospitals in the South. Even though the place was eventually torn down and replaced by a big- ass football stadium, someone had saved the wood, pews, stained glass, and other objects. The museum reassembled it here.

Dani walked to the front and studied the wood with the word *holy* in it three times, separated by crosses. An elderly couple came over, holding hands, their simple golden bands contrasting against their dark skin. As she moved across the room, she noticed the way they smiled at each other; how even though the man limped, he kept hold of his wife, looking at her like she was the only thing that mattered in the world.

The intimacy between them made her feel like she was intruding on a private moment, yet she couldn't look away. She smiled when the woman caught her eye. And then she found herself walking toward them for reasons she didn't completely understand.

"Hi," she said. "You two just look so happy, I... Well, I don't know, really. Just wanted to say keep on doing whatever you're doing." The words sounded stupid, and she wanted to rewind time and hang back instead of disturbing them.

But then the woman's eyes found hers. "We met here. Well, when the place wasn't here. This is where we fell in love..."

An hour later, Dani hesitated in front of the exit of the museum, not wanting to leave, even though she needed to get ready for the wedding. She glanced at the people at the information desk, tempted to ask them about their wedding ceremony options and how far in advance they were booked. After hearing Mr. and Mrs. Clark's love story, she really did want to get married here, so close to where they'd met and where the world was progressing, people slowly changing their minds about segregation.

Would it be weird to pick a date in about two years and just hope that I'll find someone by then?

One thing was for sure: she was done bobbing through life, having it happen to her more than making it happen.

I'm taking control. First step: promotion. Then she could focus on the rest of her life. Put herself out there, meet some friends, possibly even a guy. At least start trying.

No more being scared of moving on.

Chapter Nine

All the setting up had been done. Audrey had even come out with her hair in curlers and approved everything—including his freshly shaven face and shorter hair. Now he was just killing time, waiting for Dani to show.

Wes's brother-in-law-to-be came outside. "The bridesmaids kicked me out so I don't accidentally see my bride and jinx the whole wedding," Matthew said. "Man, I love your sister and all, but I'll be glad when the wedding's over. Don't get scared when Dani goes nutso over decorations—it's normal and then they change back. Or so I've heard. Fingers crossed," he added, raising his own fingers.

"Dani won't be like that," Wes said.

Matthew raised his eyebrows, his skepticism clear.

Wes figured there wasn't any point in arguing. Some guests started to show up, and he sat down, tapping his fingers on his thighs, anxious for Dani to hurry and get there.

What if she decided she doesn't want to keep up this fake engagement anymore? If Audrey thought his announcing he was getting married again created too much drama, he didn't want to think about how mad she'd be at Dani being a no-show. Or at his family learning the truth.

He stood, now worried she might've gotten into a wreck or something.

What if she's on her way to the hospital right now?

He ran a hand through his hair. He needed to calm down.

It would really help if his pulse wasn't thumping through his head and his tie wasn't choking him, and he hadn't worn these shoes in forever and now he was remembering why.

He pulled out his phone. No messages. Twenty minutes until the ceremony started. He should probably be inside, asking Mom if she needed any last-minute help, but he remained rooted to the spot, watching the guests arrive. Waiting for Dani to arrive.

"You okay?"

Wes turned back. Jill was dressed in the jade bridesmaid dress—not green, as he'd been told again and again—with a big white flower in her hair.

"Yeah. Fine. How's Audrey?"

"Alternatively giddy and weepy."

Wes glanced back toward the entrance. Then did a double take.

Dani *had* threatened to kill him. This must be the way she planned to do it.

Her dark hair was down around her shoulders and she was wearing earrings that glittered in the sunlight. The purple dress she had on showed off her toned legs and hugged her curves.

The supply of oxygen to his brain cut off, and he was pretty sure his heart had stopped a couple of beats ago.

"Dude, you're practically drooling." Jill patted his back. "You can go say hi, you know."

Sure. If he could remember how to walk. Dani had always been pretty, but now she was the kind of beautiful that practically hurt to look at. That pep talk he'd given himself earlier about not thinking of Dani in any way that involved her body or his was totally ineffective now.

Somehow he managed to make his feet work. He swallowed when he reached her, unable to say anything more than, "Wow."

"Wow for the backwards dress?" She twisted so he could see the draping that showed off lots of bronze skin.

His pulse cranked up a couple more notches. "I underestimated the backwards dress. Not a mistake I'll make again."

"And look at you." She reached up and ran her hand down his face. He felt her touch all the way to his toes. "You shaved."

He cleared his throat. "Figured I'd make my sister happy on her special, over-hyped day."

Dani's redder-than-normal lips curved into a smile. "Makes me happy, too. You can't use your face as a weapon anymore. How will you torture me now?"

"I'm sure I'll find something else, don't you worry."

She moved her fingers up through his hair, and everything inside him turned to mush. "No more hobo fiancé. I'm glad you didn't go too short, though. I like it a little long."

"Oh, Wes, there you are." Mom strode over to them, arms swinging. "Sorry to interrupt, but have you seen your father?" She held up a flower. "Gotta put this boutonniere on him and then I need to check on the girls and the preacher and the ceremony's getting so close and I feel like there's something else I'm forgetting." She put a hand on the top of her head and glanced around. Between her harried look and the way she was running her words together, he could tell she was starting to crack.

So despite the fact he desperately wanted to stay by Dani and finish the moment he hoped they were having, he held out his hand. "Give me the flower thing. I'll find Dad and check on the guys and the preacher." He turned to Dani, putting his hand on her hip. Tonight he was going to use any and every excuse he could to touch her. "We're sitting up near the front. You'll see the reserved chairs."

"Actually," Mom said. "I could use Dani if that's okay. My hands are shaking so badly, and it'll be good to have another set of eyes when we do the last-minute preps on Audrey and the girls."

Wes raised his eyebrows at Dani, silently asking her if it was okay. When it came to his family, she'd gone along with a lot, and he already owed her for that.

"It's fine," she said. "You go, and I'll see you in a few minutes. Save me a seat?"

Wes leaned in and whispered, "Thank you."

Then he kissed her cheek.

Because he was losing his mind, apparently.

. . .

Dani struggled to keep up with Kathleen as she rushed to the stairs. Her thoughts were still on Wes and how amazing he looked in that suit and tie. Not like it was a newsflash he was hot, but this was a new drool-worthy, forget-your-own-name level. Maybe good-looking and great personality didn't automatically equal crazy passion, but maybe that kind of romantic chemistry was horribly overrated. After all, it'd fade eventually, and wasn't it more important to be able to stand the person you were with? That would never fade with Wes.

Dani was so lost in her thoughts, she almost slammed into Kathleen when she abruptly stopped.

"I forgot to pull the stuff for the punch out of the freezer. I'm not even sure it'll thaw in time for the reception." She spun around. "I'll take care of that. Can you go in and see if the girls need anything?"

Before Dani could suggest they switch duties, Kathleen was hurrying down the stairs, muttering to herself.

Dani could hear voices coming from the door to her right. She knocked and went in.

A cloud of hairspray hung heavy in the air and there was a bustle of activity, the rustle of tulle and satin.

Audrey glanced over her shoulder at Dani. She was a vision in white satin and lace, her blond hair pinned up in curls. The next instant she was hugging Dani so tightly she thought she was going to crush her rib cage. "I'm so glad you're here." She pulled back, fanning her eyes with her hand. "Oh no, I'm going to cry again. Jill!"

Jill came over with a tissue, dabbing at her sister's eyes. "Deep breaths. I'll grab the powder and we'll touch you up, but then we need to go."

As Jill brushed past, she leaned in and whispered, "Sophie's zipper is stuck. We're not telling Audrey yet, hoping we'll get it fixed in time. Could you go see if you can get it for me while I take care of Audrey?"

Go help Sophie. Sure. Not awkward at all.

She slowly approached Sophie, who was dabbing her eyes with a tissue. Apparently everyone was crying.

Dani stared for a moment, wondering how she'd gotten roped into this. She hesitantly reached out and patted Sophie's shoulder. "It's okay. We'll get your dress fixed, no need to cry."

Sophie glanced up at her and sighed. "I'm not crying because of the dress. I'm just…" She gestured around the room. "I was supposed to be doing this in a few weeks. I was going to have the ceremony of my dreams with the man of my dreams."

An icy knot formed in Dani's stomach. "I'm sure you'll still have it someday."

"Not when the man of my dreams is with someone else." Sophie dabbed at the tears that spilled out of her eyes. "I'm sorry, that came across as bitchy. I'm not trying to be, I swear, but I didn't expect to have such a hard time with it." She took a shuddering breath. "Can you block me from Audrey so she doesn't see I'm falling apart?"

Dani moved her body between Audrey and Sophie. "I'm sorry, too. I don't know what to say." What she wanted to say was, *You dumped him and now he's mine and you can't have him.* But he *wasn't* hers, not really, and she'd suspected from the moment she'd gotten to Charlotte that part of Wes did belong to Sophie. Maybe all of him.

Needing something else to focus on, she told Sophie to turn around and then stared at the zipper. Some of the satiny green material had gotten lodged in the side. Dani gently tugged the tab up and down, but it didn't move. She was tempted to really yank, but if Sophie's dress got torn, who was going to believe it wasn't because Wes's current fiancée was jealous of his old one? Especially since it was a little true.

Dani managed to get the fabric out, but the zipper's tab would only go down, not up.

Kathleen poked her head in the room. "We're supposed to go out now. Everyone ready?"

Sophie cast a worried glance over her shoulder at Dani.

Dani, in turn, glanced around for something to help, like the answer would magically appear. The pencil on the desk caught her eye. Once, when the lock on her college apartment got stuck, Wes had come to help her fix it. He'd brought this graphite lubricant tube and put it in the lock to get the tumblers working again.

Audrey was standing up, running her hands along her skirt. Jill shot a questioning, wide-eyed look at Dani. She grabbed the pencil, rubbed it up and down the zipper, worried in the end all she'd have was a dress with gray smudges on it that still wouldn't zip.

A deep breath and then she pulled on the tab. It snagged for a second but then caught and slid up, nice and smooth. A sigh of relief escaped her lips. "Ready."

Sophie started to step forward, but then turned back and whispered, "Thank you, Dani."

It wasn't *Take care of Wes for me*, or *You're the one who's right for him*, or any of the dramatic scenes you see in the movies, but the genuineness of Sophie's voice and the sad smile sent a pang of guilt through her. She hadn't told Wes that there was no reason to get over the girl he wasn't over. But she needed to.

After she told him, he'd probably want to go declare his love to Sophie and kiss her, right then and there, which would be confusing, since everyone thought he was engaged to her.

Wes and I have gotten ourselves into a royal mess this time.

• • •

Wes kept glancing at Dani during the ceremony. She'd told him everything was fine when he asked, but now she was twisting her "engagement ring" around her finger, the diamond winking in the sunlight every time it got to the top.

He reached over and took her hand, lacing his fingers with hers. She looked at him—she'd done something to her eyes to make them stand out even more, the purple highlighting the dark brown of her irises, and his stomach twisted just looking at her. It was like a switch had been flipped and there was no way to turn it off now. Damn, he was falling.

Falling for his best friend.

It would've been a good thing if he didn't know that she'd never fall for him back.

He swallowed his feelings, a bitter taste in his mouth, and

returned his attention to Audrey and Matthew, reciting their vows in front of the preacher.

Then there were the *I Do*s and the pronouncing of man and wife. They kissed and the audience cheered.

Mom swiped tears from her cheeks, then leaned over, smiling at him and Dani. "You two are next."

Wes was saved from having to respond to that by everyone standing for the couple as they walked back down the aisle, hand in hand. Then people headed over to the reception area, and it was a blur of movement, caterers filling drinks and bringing food, and dozens of conversations filling the air.

Dani was quiet, and for the first time in years, he had no idea what to say to her. Finally, he decided to go for simple. "You okay?"

She set down her water glass, nodded, and then poked at the chicken on her plate with her fork.

Geez, it's like pulling teeth. He talked to Mom and Dad for a couple of minutes, then glanced at Dani again.

"Do anything interesting this morning?"

"I went to the Levine Museum, actually," she said.

"Let me guess where you spent the most time. The Good Samaritan Chapel."

Finally he got a smile. "You know me too well. And the most amazing thing happened in there." Her face lit up as she told him about the couple she'd met at the museum.

Wes squeezed her hand. "You put on a tough front, Dani Vega, but then you almost cry over a couple's love story."

She frowned at him. "I wasn't about to cry." One shoulder lifted in a half shrug. "But it was a lovely story." She dropped her fork and leaned in, keeping her voice low. "I guess it just got me thinking... And then I see your parents, and how Jill and her husband are, not to mention Audrey and Matthew, and I know it's stupid but..." She shook her head. "Never mind."

"What?" He tugged on her hand until she looked at him again.

"Sometimes I worry I won't ever have that. My mom was alone for most of her life. Yes, she had me, and now she has my abuela, but that's different. And I don't have a kid or even a pet." She shrugged again, like it was no big deal, but he could hear in her voice that she was genuinely worried. "Just ignore me. I guess I'm not immune to getting emotional at weddings."

Now the sun was setting, and the white lights Mom had him drape everywhere yesterday were on, softly lighting Dani's features. He held her gaze for a moment, then put his elbow on the table and moved closer to her. "No matter what happens or who comes into our lives, we'll always have each other. Whatever you need. Whenever. Even if I've got to come with a cane or a walker."

One of her eyebrows arched higher than the other. "What if you end up married to a girl who hates me?" she whispered.

"Even then," he said, firm, not bothering to whisper back. "She accepts that you're part of my life or she's not a part of mine."

Dani's eyes shone with unshed tears, and his chest tightened. She blinked quickly and smiled. "If I ever have a boyfriend again, the same rule applies to him."

If. Like she'd have trouble finding someone.

The microphone squealed and Jill took it to deliver her maid of honor toast. Matthew's college buddy followed, making his toast, and then Audrey and Matthew had their first dance as husband and wife.

When the next song started up, Wes stood and held out his hand to Dani. "Come dance with me."

Her hand slipped into his, like it was meant to be there, and he led her onto the floor with the other couples. She hooked her fingers behind his neck and swayed to the music.

Figuring he could get away with dancing close, he slid his arms tighter around her waist until there wasn't any space between them.

He could feel her chest rise and fall against his, and the rest of the dance party faded away to a blur. Being here with her was no longer about making anyone jealous or keeping his family off his case. It was about having her in his arms and soaking in every moment while he could. "I've had so much fun the past few days; I don't want to think about the fact that I have to go home tomorrow," she said.

Wes exhaled a shaky breath. "Me neither." *I want you to stay forever.* He'd avoided commitment or even dating the last few months, so the thought surprised him. But it was true. He didn't realize how much he'd missed her since she moved away, and now he didn't want to let her go back to Arkansas.

She reached up and ran her hand down his cheek again. "Still can't get over this."

If she were going to do that every time he shaved, he'd start doing it every day. Obviously she didn't know what she was doing to him. He had to start silently listing state capitals in his head to keep himself under control. He definitely shouldn't be thinking about how amazing her body felt pressed against his.

He moved his hands, grazing the soft skin on her back. The backwards dress suddenly became his favorite thing *ever.*

Dani looked up into his eyes, and he wondered for a heart-stopping second if she were going to ask what he was doing and pull away.

But then she dropped her head on his shoulder. He soaked in the moment, inhaling her perfume and daring to brush his fingers across her skin again. "Can we just freeze this moment for a while?" she asked.

Wes barely resisted the urge to kiss the top of her head. He could probably play it off as acting, but could he do it without then tipping her chin up and kissing her for real?

The music cut off, and he'd never despised the ending of a song so much. Dani lifted her head, her body still pressed against his. Something flickered through her gaze and his posture tensed.

"Wes, I need to tell you something."

"Everyone!" The screech of the microphone shattered the silence. Audrey stood up front, her arm around her brand-new husband. "Matthew and I just want to thank you all for coming. Planning a wedding involved more than I ever knew it would, and I just want to thank my family for helping me pull off such a beautiful one. We've always been very close, and they mean the world to me. And that includes my brother and my sister-in-law-to-be. Dani, Wes, come up here."

Dani stiffened.

Audrey waved toward them. "Come on, you guys. Get up here already."

• • •

The last thing Dani wanted was to go up there. But everyone was already staring at her and Wes, and she wasn't sure what else to do. She gripped his hand, taking comfort in the way his fingers automatically wrapped around hers.

The crowd parted as they made their way to the podium in front, where the band was set up and Audrey was holding the mic. Wes led her to the stage, and she could feel heat crawling up her neck and into her face.

Her hands ached to have a basketball in them. Something to distract her from all the stares. Audrey grinned, radiating happiness. "Now when my brother brought his new fiancée home, I was so wrapped up in my own stuff, I'm afraid I didn't give her a proper welcome into our family. So I wanted to propose a toast." She lifted a fluted glass. "To Wes and

Dani. May your dreams all come true, like mine have today."

The crowd responded with *hear, hear*, echoing the toast.

Dani spotted Kathleen in the crowd, beaming up at them.

Look how happy she is. She's going to hate me when she finds out Wes and I aren't getting married. But then he'll get back together with Sophie and they'll all get over it. Tears pricked her eyes and she swallowed a lump in her throat.

Except me.

Audrey thrust the mic toward Wes.

He shook his head and whispered, "It's your day."

"I know, and I want you to say something." She practically jabbed it into his nose.

Wes reluctantly took the mic. He glanced at Dani, at his parents, and then his eyes drifted over the rest of the crowd.

Dani noticed Sophie standing off to the side, face pale. Back on the dance floor, she'd been about to tell Wes exactly how his ex felt, but this speech had cut her off. Now she worried it was going to ruin any shot they had at getting back together, and it would be all her fault. But what was she supposed to do? Take the mic and tell everyone this wasn't real and that he belonged with Sophie? Maybe if this were a movie and she were a better person, but there was no way in hell she was doing that.

Wes lifted the mic to his mouth and turned on the charm for the crowd. "First of all, I want to say congrats to Audrey and Matthew. I know you guys are going to have a great life together. Just remember to have some adventures along the way, so the stress of everyday life doesn't get you down." He looked at his sister and smiled, the affection in his eyes clear. "Take some chances once in a while. Do something impulsive. No getting boring on me."

Audrey raised an eyebrow, but she was smiling back at Wes. She gave a little nod.

"As for Dani..." Wes let go of her hand and slid his arm

around her waist. "She's been my best friend for a long time. And I..." His eyes locked onto hers and her heart caught. "I love her like crazy, and I'm so glad she said yes."

*Aww*s went through the audience.

Audrey took the microphone, held it down, and then whispered. "Kiss her already. And don't be a wuss about it."

Wes turned to face her, and her pulse hammered through her ears. All these people. Watching them kiss. *Don't think about the weirdness or the fact that we suck at kissing. Just sell it for the audience. And at least he shaved so I won't get whisker burn this time.*

He leaned down and gently pressed his lips to hers. She was about to pull back, figuring they'd put on a good enough show, when he pulled her flush against him and parted her lips with his. Then she was gripping the sides of his waist, fire blazing a trail from her lips to her core as she kissed him back.

He dipped her slightly, his tongue ran across the top of her lip, and then he eased her back up. She wobbled, grabbing onto his arm to keep from falling over. It was just a result of wearing heels for so long, she told herself. And that kiss was all for show...

But that show had resulted in her tingling lips and the inability to catch her breath. *Okay, not quite like last time.*

Wes's eyes were glued to hers. She glanced away, unable to deal with the confusing emotions swirling through her, and took a large step off the stage. People patted her shoulder and congratulated her as she passed.

Kathleen threw her arms around her, enveloping her in a hug so tight she could hardly breathe. "I'm so glad it was you," she said.

Air. All this open space and there was no air. Her lungs were straining for it and her head was spinning. She smiled the best she could manage and then pushed out of the crowd as fast as she could without running.

The music swelled and conversations rose again. She stumbled over a stone and cursed her shoes. She braced herself against the closest tree and took a couple of deep breaths.

A moment later, she felt a hand on her arm and turned.

"My kiss was that bad, huh?" Wes said it like a joke, but it didn't carry his usual cocky flare.

He was worried he was a sucky kisser, and right now she thought he was too good of one.

Since she wasn't sure how to go there without leaving her heart exposed, in too much danger of being crushed, she paved over the statement with, "Your mom's going to be so hurt when we tell her we broke up." Dani bit her lip. "I know it's not fair of me to ask for you to lie to your family forever, but please don't tell her it was all fake."

"I'll tell her that we decided we were better off as friends," he said. "She'll be fine."

Dani gave him a look to show him how much she doubted that.

"Okay, you're right." He ran a hand through his hair. "We really didn't think this through. I should've known my mom would fall in love with you. You want to leave? I can make up an excuse."

"I'm fine. I just needed some air. Not used to the crowd and the attention." *And the kissing. If you'd kissed me like that the first time, I never would've been with anyone else.*

And suddenly she knew no matter who she met, who she kissed, she'd forever compare them to the kiss he'd given her tonight, after telling everyone he loved her.

Just like she knew, without a doubt, they'd all fall short.

Chapter Ten

Dani leaned against the deck railing and covered a yawn. The bride and groom had driven away in their streamer-covered car and all of the wedding and reception guests were gone. The sun had set a while ago and the night was the perfect temperature.

Days of setup—months of work, really—and an hour after the reception, there was only a beat-up lawn and giant bins full of trash to show for it. No more tables or chairs or decorations, just a couple of strings of twinkling white lights. She tried not to think about it, because it only reminded her that soon she'd be headed back to her real life, this night only a memory.

And that was where the kiss from Wes would be, too. A keepsake of a perfect night where they'd laughed, danced close, and shared one magical moment, even if she was the only one who'd felt the magic.

Wes came over, tie hanging loose and the top few buttons of his shirt undone. His wavy blond hair was slightly disheveled in a completely sexy way. "That took longer than I expected." He glanced at his watch. "The rest of the band's probably already setting up, wondering where I am. We're going to have to rush to get to the show. I don't think we even have time to change."

Dani straightened. "This is what I always wear to concerts, anyway. I'm fancy like that."

"Well, come on then, Miss Fancy Pants." He put his hand on the small of her back and led her inside. When he passed by the dining room where his mom was sitting with Jill, a mess of centerpieces filling the table, he said, "Dani and I have to go."

Kathleen got to her feet. "Are you sure? You know, both of you could stay here tonight. I could make up a room for Dani, and you could sleep in the—"

"Thanks, Mom," Wes said. "But I've got a show and it'll be late." He glanced at Dani and mouthed, *You owe me five bucks.*

She didn't admit it was the second time Kathleen had offered to have her stay. His mom hugged him, then turned to her and enveloped her in a hug, crushing her mother-of-the-bride corsage between them.

"I'm so happy you came, and I'll be in touch to talk wedding details." Kathleen dropped her arms but didn't step away, just stared at her for a beat. "You two are going to have such beautiful children."

"Mom," Wes said, a warning in his voice.

"What? No pressure, but I'm just saying eventually—"

"Night, Mom." Wes nodded at his sister. "Jill. Catch you later."

They waved and exchanged a few more good-byes before getting out the door. A pang went through Dani when she realized she might be walking away from this house for the last time. A lump even formed in her throat.

Man, what's with me today?

As an only child who'd lost her father so early in life, she'd always envied people with big families. Even though

Steve had two brothers and they'd visited his parents a couple of times, his family had never taken her in and made her feel like part of them. In fact, she always felt temporary—and it turned out she was.

Over the past few days, she'd almost felt like she was part of Wes's family, and she didn't want to let it go. She cast one last glance over her shoulder, taking a moment to remember the beautiful stone archway, flowerbeds, and perfectly sculpted shrubs and trees. She held the image of when Wes first walked her inside and there were people everywhere and his niece and nephew ran up to him. Just for a second, she let herself imagine it was all real—that she was engaged to the perfect guy and was about to be married into the family she'd grown to love in such a short amount of time.

Then she took a deep breath, let the image cloud over, and blew it away until only a wisp of the memories and the yearning in her body remained.

Wes opened the car door for her. Her eyes ran across his chest and up to his face. She wanted to run her hand down his cheek again—hell, she wanted to feel his lips against hers again. Earlier he'd promised they'd always have each other, and he obviously meant it as friends. So even if she couldn't have the rest—his family and his heart—she'd hold on to that.

And hope to God that Sophie would accept her so that it could be true.

• • •

The streetlights flashed across Dani's face, lighting it up one moment and leaving it in darkness the next.

Traffic got heavier as they headed out of his parents' neighborhood. "Sorry about my mom and that whole kids thing."

Dani ran her fingers along the bottom of the passenger

door window. "It's okay."

He was tempted to say, *For the record, our kids* would *be beautiful*, but he'd obviously freaked her out with that kiss already.

That kiss was… He didn't even know what to call it. He hadn't meant to do more than give her a peck, but then his lips were against hers and he'd stopped thinking and just gone for it. It had almost been better when he *didn't* know what it was like to really kiss her.

At least he didn't remember the drunken kiss. The one tonight was going to be seared into his mind forever. His gaze went to those lips again.

She tensed. "Wes, the light's red."

He glanced up and hit the brakes, managing to stop them from barreling into the intersection, but *damn* that was close.

Dani was holding onto the bar over the door. "I know you're used to flying in the open air, but when we drive on the roads, there are things like stoplights."

"Yeah, for the tight-asses who follow rules like that," he said, attempting a joke even though his stomach had relocated to his throat. The light turned green and he eased through the intersection, hands gripping the steering wheel and eyes fixed on the road. He had to readjust his thinking back to Dani being his friend and nothing more.

A few more minutes and he was pulling up behind the bar. Light spilled out of the back door, and he could see the outline of the guys already unloading the equipment. He parked next to the van, got out, and grabbed his guitar from the trunk. He frowned down at his clothes. "I don't look very rock and roll."

Dani pursed her lips as she ran her eyes over him. She ducked inside the car and brought out his aviator shades. "Will it be too dark to play in these?"

"I think I can manage." He put them on while she undid his tie and slid it off. Then she reached up and tousled his hair, her body bumping against his. He took a deep breath of whatever intoxicating perfume she was wearing, suppressing a groan at the feel of her fingers in his hair.

Her hand slid down, resting on his chest, and he wondered if she could feel his rapid heartbeat. "You look good. With or without the shades."

He meant to say thanks but his mouth wasn't working.

"Wes? You coming or what?"

Wes glanced at Rob and Paul, standing by the door. "Yeah. Just having my stylist fix my wardrobe." He was about to reach for Dani's hand when he remembered they weren't pretending to be engaged anymore. He settled for putting his hand on her back and leading her over to the guys.

"You met Paul already, and this is Rob. Rob, Dani."

Wes didn't like the way Paul was staring at her, his mouth practically hanging open. "Hi again," he said.

Wes stepped between her and the guys. "Anything else we need to do to set up?"

"Nah, you got here just in time," Rob said.

They went to the miniscule back room where the band could lounge—if lounging included sitting on a smoky-smelling couch and a couple of recliners that no longer reclined. He'd always liked the room, though. Something about it got him in the mindset to go onstage and get lost in the music and the energy from the audience, even if there were only fifty or so people in the bar and only half of them were paying attention.

He flipped open his guitar case and took out his Gibson Firebird. He strummed a few chords, then looked up, figuring he'd chat with Dani or try to make her laugh.

Instead, she was talking to Paul. He had her hand in his, and a toxic, burning sensation traveled through Wes's veins. He took off his sunglasses so he could see better, then sort of wished he hadn't.

"That's my ring, you know," Paul said. "Guess that makes you engaged to me now." He laughed like it was a hilarious joke, and Dani smiled at him.

"Well, I go wherever the ring takes me. Not because I'm a gold digger or anything; it's more of a Lord of the Rings thing. This ring gives me powers. Though I'm totally going to lose it when my hair falls out and I start calling it 'my precious.'"

Paul got a big kick out of that.

The burning sensation spread. Wes tried to calm down—tried to tell himself that in all honesty, he wanted her to find a good guy, and Paul was a good guy.

But he was still happy when he realized it didn't really matter. Dani was leaving tomorrow, so she and Paul would never work.

Of course, that meant neither would he and Dani.

Someone in Arkansas would be taking her out, making her laugh. Kissing her.

The toxic burn grew with a vengeance.

· · ·

The first few songs were nice and mellow—perfect *sit back and have a drink at a bar* music. But it gave Dani way too much time to stare at Wes, no fear of him catching her. The way his face scrunched up in concentration when the faster part of the song came. How the muscles in his forearms stood out as he played his guitar.

How a mixture of burning lust and icy fear wound through her, leaving her hot and cold and confused as hell.

Or maybe the problem was that she *wasn't* confused. His kiss had made things all too clear. She wanted him to kiss her again.

But then what?

She would go back home. He would get back with his ex.

At least one of them would get to be with whom they wanted.

All she had to do was tell him about Sophie.

And she would.

Eventually.

The song ended, and applause went through the crowd. Dani put her fingers in her mouth and whistled, earning her dirty looks from the girls close by.

Wes glanced at her and grinned, so she could care less about the dirty looks. He stepped forward and whispered something to Rob, then took the microphone and looked her way, a mischievous expression on his face.

Her stomach clenched.

Wes's mischievous grin widened, and she knew she wasn't going to like what came out of his mouth. "Tonight we have a special guest, and she's agreed to sing for us."

Surely he doesn't mean me. He'd have to be—

"Dani, why don't you come up onstage?"

She crossed her arms and shook her head.

A spotlight swung toward where she stood, practically blinding her. People cheered, yelling for her to get onstage.

Cursing Wes and definitely not feeling the lust anymore, she strode to the front. Wes reached out a hand and helped her up. She tugged down her skirt as she stared at the audience. The place was half full, but with all eyes on her, it felt like a sold-out arena.

She glared at Wes.

He leaned down, his breath hitting her neck. "I know, I know. You're going to kill me." He straightened and lifted the mic. "I'm just giving her a hard time. I wanted you all to see that I'm here with the hottest girl in the room."

She stared at him, wondering why he was doing this. Yes, he was all about being charming and the center of attention, but calling her the hottest girl in the room? It felt like he was toying with her emotions.

"I won't make her sing, but I wanted you all to meet her. This girl is one of the coolest people I know. She's been my best friend since college, and I just..." He took her hand and lowered the mic, leaving them alone in a room full of people. "I don't know where I'd be without you. I'm going to miss you like crazy."

The air shifted, too thin and too heavy at the same time. She hugged him tightly, choking back the tears crawling up her throat.

There was only one thing to do now.

Go out on a high note. Literally.

She took the mic from him and his eyebrows shot up. "You boys know 'My Life Would Suck Without You' by Kelly Clarkson?" she asked. Of course she knew Wes did, but she wasn't sure if he'd let his band mates in on his Kelly obsession. Both that and the title made it the perfect pick for her. Paul and Rob glanced at each other and nodded. Wes gave her one last look—she wasn't sure if he thought she was crazy or he was worried she was about to send their set crashing and burning. In all honesty, she wasn't sure, either.

She hadn't sung for anyone since high school. But she'd practiced plenty, dancing and singing around her apartment when she was alone. Her throat tightened and the blood rushed through her head so fast it made her dizzy.

The music started and she tried not to think about all the people currently staring at her. The first few words came out shaky, with not nearly enough volume, but then she let the music take over and belted out the lyrics. Once she felt in control, she moved over to Wes, leaning against him as she sang, like the pop stars did at their concerts.

When the song ended, people cheered, and her Rock Star For a Night dream was fulfilled. She handed the mic back to Wes.

"I guess the joke's on me," he said, his words barely

discernible through all the cheering. "I didn't know you could sing."

She leaned in so that she was pressed against him. "There are a lot of things you don't know about me," she said in her most seductive voice.

He looked down at her and swallowed. If they kissed again right now, would it be real? Or would it still be for show?

Did it matter if it destroyed everything?

Wes ran his fingers down her arm and took her hand. Her skin hummed underneath his touch, and she wasn't sure she was breathing anymore.

"Thanks to Dani for helping out," Rob said, his loud voice making her jump. "We've got time for one more song, and then we'll leave you guys till next week."

In other words, *Dani get off the stage so we can finish*.

She smiled at Wes, though it wasn't easy to pull off, and jumped from the stage. The sudden heat in the place was stifling. For the second time that night, she needed air. Leaving the swelling noise of the last song behind, she pushed out the front door. The cool breeze drifted across her clammy skin, a welcome change. But it snapped her thoughts into focus, too.

Kissing him again would've been a mistake.
Right?

Part of her wanted to stay in Charlotte forever, but another part of her was glad she was leaving tomorrow, because she couldn't take her yo-yo-ing emotions anymore. She needed to focus on the future. What was real. She had responsibilities. A job with a promotion on the line that could help ease her and her family's financial burdens. Her life wasn't here. Not anymore.

Probably not ever again.

If only that thought didn't give her a choking sense of

desperation.

. . .

Wes packed up his guitar, flipping the case closed with a satisfying *click*. Paul was still over talking to Dani, like he had been since they'd gotten offstage. He was still praising her singing.

And he was right. Dani had an amazing voice.

Had he imagined that moment onstage when she'd delivered that line—it was a flirty line, right? Did that mean his attraction to her wasn't one-sided? If he'd misread it, making a move could screw up everything. But if he did nothing, he might regret it forever.

Then again, she might be talking to Paul forever.

"Hey, you want to go get a drink?" Paul asked her. "Or we could just go to my place and hang out for a while."

Wes's insides revolted at the thought of Paul taking her home. Suddenly, he had to fight the urge to take a swing at one of his best friends. His mind started coming up with excuses why she shouldn't—couldn't—go. But he wasn't her dad, and if she wanted to...

Shit, what if she wants to?

He couldn't hear what she said, but then she leaned in and hugged Paul.

Every muscle in Wes's body tensed.

Then she called out a good-bye to Rob, waved at Paul, and stepped toward him. His blood cooled and his body relaxed. She was coming home with him. He picked up his guitar and put his other hand on her back. "Ready?"

She nodded.

They got into his car and started down the road. As much as he wanted to stare at her, he decided he probably shouldn't almost run any more red lights.

She kicked off her shoes and tucked one of her legs up. "I probably should've gone with Paul. I haven't had a cute guy ask me out in a while." She looked at him. Did she really want a response to that? He *should* tell her Paul was a great guy, but the words stayed lodged in his throat.

He exhaled, deciding to leave Paul out of it. "You would have guys all over you if you wore that dress all the time."

"My backwards dress? Or do I need to turn it around so my boobs are hanging out?"

Holy shit. She really *was* trying to kill him. Now he was thinking about her boobs and he had to shift in his seat.

She glanced at him, her cheeks flushed. "Just pretend I didn't say that."

Easier said than done.

"All I was saying was…" She dropped her head in her hands. "I don't know anymore."

All I'm saying is you don't need to find another guy. I'll be that guy. He wanted to have the balls to say it. But if she were even thinking about going home with Paul, he *had* misread her. And either way, it didn't change the fact that she was leaving tomorrow. And they were supposed to be pretend-engaged again in two weeks.

Better to wait and see what happened then.

In theory.

• • •

Dani kicked her shoes off as soon as they stepped inside Wes's apartment. She considered flopping onto the couch, but the odds weren't good she'd get up again if she did. Her feet ached all the way to her bones, and her muscles were too tight.

Not to mention it was almost two a.m., and she had a plane to catch at the butt crack of dawn. When she'd booked the flight, she'd been thinking she'd get an early one so she could catch up on work and be ready for Monday morning. Now she was thinking she'd give anything for a few more hours with Wes, even if they were just talking about nothing until the sun rose, the way they used to do in college.

She looked up to find him watching her. He glanced away. "So…?"

"I've got an early flight."

"Yeah."

"I should probably get some sleep." She waited to see if he'd stop her. She wanted him to. It caused a feather of fear, thinking about taking that risk with Wes, but the thrill of how great it might be was mixed in there, too.

He nodded. "Right. Well, I'll set my alarm on my phone in case you don't hear yours."

She smiled. "It happens all the time. I've even had to move my alarm right next to me. I think I need one that shoots water or something."

"I think I'd scour the world to find one of those only so I could be there the first time it woke you up."

That brought an image of waking up with him in her bed. Or his bed. Didn't really matter. She waited a beat longer, pointed in the direction of his hallway, like he'd be so confused if she simply walked down it first, then took slow steps toward his bedroom.

To her surprise, Wes followed her. She spun around in the doorway.

"Thanks for coming," he said. "The engagement thing aside, I've had a blast."

Wait. Is he saying pretending to be engaged wasn't fun? Or is he saying… Hell, I don't know what he means.

Time and time again, she'd heard that you should just tell a guy what you want. That they're not mind readers—as if they're not cryptic or hard to understand, either.

So what do I want?

Her eyes drank him in again. The pale blue eyes, five o'clock shadow, and rumpled shirt. Her body heated as she thought about the muscles he was hiding under that button-down. Her fingers twitched at her sides, wanting to be bold enough to reach up and undo one button at a time.

She tried to swallow, but her throat was too dry.

Would it be so bad, just for tonight, to have his body pressed against hers? It'd been a while since she'd been with anyone. And if she was going to get back in the game, she might as well get a jump-start with someone she knew she could trust, even if it was only one night.

One night before he found out about Sophie and he wasn't hers anymore.

"Dani?" Her name came out a whisper from his lips.

Her heart squeezed, her blood rushed through her veins, and she could feel herself coming undone. He made her forget her fears. Made her a little reckless.

But there was reckless and then there was stupid. How could she get over a night of casual sex with him? It'd ruin everything they'd built over the years. She was stronger than that.

He stepped closer, eradicating the space between them, and cupped her cheek. Her resolve unraveled.

Then he leaned forward and gave her other cheek a peck, similar to the ones he'd given her this week. "Good night."

A scratchy "good night" left her mouth.

He turned and walked away. With every step, a string in her heart tugged.

She told herself it was for the best.

But it didn't feel like the best.

It felt like falling apart, one piece at a time.

Chapter Eleven

The ride to the airport somehow managed to be too fast and too slow, too quiet and too loud. Wes changed lanes, grumbled when the car ahead of him was barely moving, and changed lanes again. Last night he'd practically made a move. Dani had frozen, something he vaguely remembered her doing the first time he'd kissed her.

This morning she was quiet, probably worried he'd try again. He wanted to say something about how tired he'd been or make a comment about how crazy last night was. But he hoped she was too tired to remember and didn't want to remind her if she actually didn't.

He'd avoided dating so he wouldn't have to question every move he made, and now here he was, more screwed up than ever. As soon as he dropped her off, he was going to get in a helicopter and fly far away from everything and everyone. Then he'd get his head straight.

Dani tucked her hair behind her ear, and that one rebellious section immediately fell forward, the way it always did. "Last night, I…"

Wes tensed, terrified of the next words out of her mouth.

She shifted in her seat to face him. "I never got to tell you that I've had a great time with you, too. I'm even considering smuggling you to Arkansas in my suitcase. You can hold your breath for three or four hours, right?"

He laughed, the stress filling his body easing. "Give or take a few hours."

The tension in her features lifted. The signs for the airport listed off the airlines and which lane to get in for each of them. "You want me to park and come in with you? Help check your bag and all that?"

She shook her head. "I'll be fine."

He veered toward the departures area, pulled up to the curb, and put the car in park. He wanted to move his hand to her knee, but they were finally back to normal. He couldn't jeopardize that. "Two weeks and I'll be coming to see you. By the time I'm done laying on the charm, the promotion will be all yours."

"If anyone can charm my way in, I'm sure it's you."

He reached for the door handle so he could grab her bag for her.

"Wes?" She put her hand on his arm and he froze. The tension was back in her posture and he silently swore. "I have to tell you something. About Sophie."

Her tension transferred to him, coiling his insides into a tight knot. "What about her?"

Dani took a deep breath, her chest rising and falling. "She still loves you. And I know you still love her."

"I don't," he said, frustration rising up in him. How many times did he have to say it before people finally got it?

She pressed her lips together. "I know I said I didn't want your family to know our engagement was a lie, but I think you should tell Sophie. You two should try to work it out."

He opened his mouth to protest again, but she cut him

off.

"Just think about it. You owe it to her and to yourself to see if there's something still there."

He was sure there wasn't, not with the way he felt about the girl sitting in the car with him. But if she felt the same, she wouldn't be telling him to pursue his ex.

Now he was more confused than ever.

"I'll help however I can," Dani said. "Even if it means you can't come to my company retreat with me."

Oh, no. He wasn't going to let her cancel on him, not when everything between them was so up in the air right now. "I'm coming," he firmly said. Maybe he hadn't been clear enough on how much she meant to him, whether or not that kiss last night meant the same to her as it did to him. "I meant what I said at the wedding. It's you and me, no matter who else comes into our lives."

"That's probably not the best decision if we ever want to move on and have healthy relationships. Think about it. I know I caused problems with you two, just like our friendship has always bugged every guy I ever dated."

He lowered his eyebrows, staring at the steering wheel. "It sounds like you're breaking up with me."

"You know I could *never* do that." She sighed. "I...I just want you to be happy. I should've told you a few days ago, after Sophie talked to me. And again at the wedding, when she told me how much she regretted breaking it off with you."

He waited to feel the warm satisfaction. Instead he felt hollow.

"And eventually, I'm going to find a guy, too," she said. "So don't worry about me. I'll be fine."

He gritted his teeth, fighting the urge to slam his fist into the steering wheel.

"I gotta go." She leaned across the seat and hugged him. There was too much space between them. Too much unsaid.

He hugged her back. If his whiskers were longer, he'd have brushed them against her cheek to hear her squeal. To have a chance to be that close again.

She started out of the car and then lifted her hand. "The ring. I forgot."

"It's better if you just keep it till I get there," Wes said. "And I *am* coming, okay? No matter what else happens, I'm helping you get that job."

"But if it—"

"Still going to show up, so you might as well get used to the idea."

The dimple in her cheek flashed. "Okay. Until then." She grabbed her bag out of the back, waved, and she was gone, the doors to the airport closing behind her.

The immediate sense of loss was déjà vu, reminding him of when they'd said good-bye the first time she went to Arkansas. All those feelings echoed through him again. The squeeze in his chest, the loneliness pressing against his skin. Like he'd never get her back and his life would always be worse for it.

Only now the pain was sharper, more a stabbing than a pressing. It felt like she'd taken all the happiness, all the oxygen, with her.

He'd meant what he said about always being there for her, no matter what. But what happened when she found a good guy who saw how awesome she was? When she didn't need to call him for advice and she was busy being in love with someone else?

I'll probably be the one to end up alone.

He scrubbed a hand across his face; now he was turning into a sap. Must be lack of sleep. He let out a breath, allowing himself to think on what Dani had told him about Sophie. A few months ago—maybe even a few weeks ago—he might've considered giving it another shot. Now he didn't know what to do.

Sophie or Dani? Where to put his focus?

If Dani had shown any signs of wanting him...

Or if she wasn't a couple of states away...

Or a hundred other ifs.

But say Sophie *did* want him. And she did live here. They'd almost made it work before, and he did still care about her. Enough to try again, though?

The security guard patrolling the lanes gave Wes a pointed look he took to mean *You've exceeded your time limit*. Wes made a big show of putting his car in gear. But before merging into traffic, he got out his phone and scrolled to Sophie's name.

• • •

Dani dropped her suitcase and laptop bag the second she entered her apartment; her neck ached from carrying everything through two airports. She tossed the mail she'd brought up from her box onto the coffee table—lots and lots of bills—and flopped onto the couch in her very silent place. She almost wished for a ticking clock just to fill the silence. Anything to keep her company.

Guess I should check my e-mails and catch up on work stuff. With a groan, she got off the couch, grabbed her laptop, and settled back down on the cushions. Two days of not checking her inbox and there was more than one page could hold. Work stuff. A couple of online sites where she frequently shopped telling her about deals. Not a single personal e-mail in the bunch.

Over the next few hours she clicked through message after message, took care of the urgent business, and typed up a to-do list for tomorrow, squeezing in tasks between meetings. She called Mama to check in, and even got to talk to Abuela, who sounded more upbeat than she had in a long time, though Dani could still hear the wheeze in her voice.

And then there was the silence again. No Wes to hang out with. No adventure waiting just around the corner.

This is my life.

My life sucks.

I need to change my life.

No more being the lonely pathetic girl who never did anything but go to work. Time to follow through on what she said she would and put herself out there. She just needed to figure out how exactly to do that. Going to a bar to wait and see if she just so happened to meet someone cool wasn't going to work, especially not all alone. She didn't want to be the sad girl dying for any random guy to talk to her. There were always dating sites—her junk mail folder was full of them. But she wasn't going to use any service that spammed her, on principle. Plus, most of them had icky names.

So she searched dating sites, found one that looked promising, and spent an hour filling out dozens of questions. By the end, she'd discovered things about herself she hadn't even known, and she wasn't sure she'd wanted to know.

She closed her laptop, and the light caught the large diamond on her finger. It was probably time to take off the ring, considering she'd just spent so much time and money on trying to find someone new to date.

Her phone beeped. A text from Wes, checking in on her.

She sent a text back, telling him she was home. She wanted to ask if he'd talked to Sophie yet but held back. He'd tell her in his own time. And honestly, she wasn't ready for the news that he wasn't hers anymore.

Her phone chimed again.

Wes: I MISS YOU ALREADY.

Warmth filled her chest, and a giant lump formed in her throat.

Another chime.

Wes: ALL MY OTHER FRIENDS ARE BORING. NO ONE ELSE WILL GO RIDE THE BULL WITH ME OR BUST INTO KELLY CLARKSON SONGS.

Dani: WELL, I AM PRETTY SPECIAL LIKE THAT :)

Wes: YES YOU ARE. PLUS YOU'RE A LOT PRETTIER TO LOOK AT.

She stared at the text, feeling that annoying squeeze in her chest. She didn't know how to respond—was he flirting? Finally, she just decided to respond with the truth.

Dani: I MISS YOU, TOO.

She glanced at her open laptop and noticed a new message in her inbox. It was from the dating site, so she figured it'd be verifying her subscription. Instead, it was a message from a guy asking her a couple of getting-to-know-you-type questions.

Well, that was fast. This online dating thing might actually work out.

So even though she did miss Wes like crazy, it was time to put him back in the friendship box and prove to herself there were other fish in the sea. Or at least other reasonably-attractive-according-to-a-most-likely-doctored-picture men who wanted to get to know her.

She sent a message back, answering his questions and asking more about him.

The possibility of moving on and starting a new chapter in her life should've made her feel empowered. So why did she feel like curling into a ball on her couch and crying?

Chapter Twelve

Moving on sucked.

Why did I think actually meeting this guy would be a good idea?

Now she was sitting in some bar she'd never been to before, all alone, looking desperately at the faces of every man who passed, wondering if he were her date for the night. Or maybe just for the hour. If it was really awful, it might even be more like five minutes. She couldn't believe she was freaking paying thirty bucks a month for this torture.

She didn't want to start all over again.

She wanted to go back to her quiet apartment and call Wes. Wanted to hear his voice and tell him about her pathetic attempt at online dating. He'd cheer her up and the world would be better, even if she wasn't technically moving on from anything.

"Danielle?"

Dani glanced in the direction the deep voice had come from. And then lifted her gaze up and up some more. As she'd learned in the messages they'd sent back and forth over the last few days, basketball was one of their common interests. Whereas she was a short guard, good from the three-point line, this guy looked like the kind of player who'd post up near the basket. Tall, dark skin, killer grin.

Moving on rocked.

She stood and offered him what she hoped was her most winning smile. "I prefer Dani, actually." Something she had mentioned in the e-mails they'd exchanged, but she supposed she could let it slide. "You must be Darryl."

"Yup." He tipped his head toward the bar. "Let's go get that drink."

From there, it went pretty smoothly. Talk mixed with some pauses as she tried to figure out what to say next. It'd been a while since she'd been on a first date. Along with the breaks in conversation and not knowing what to say, though, there was that glimmer of hope for what could be.

Maybe those dating websites did know what they were doing.

Dani's phone rang, and "SexyBack" filled the air. As nice as this date was going, her fingers still itched to answer and talk to Wes. With catching up at work and sending messages to Darryl, she'd been busy, and he must've been, too, because they hadn't talked since Sunday. After several days together, five days of no communication felt like a lifetime.

She glanced at Darryl. *It'd be rude to answer, and I don't want him to get the wrong idea.*

She hit the button to send the call to voice mail.

"Interesting ringtone," he said, a smile tipping his lips.

"It's…" She cut herself off. Wes would come up eventually if she kept dating Darryl, but it was a little too early to bring up that situation, especially considering the song, and especially since he'd be playing her fiancé again in a week. She took a sip of her drink. "So you were saying you played ball in college, too. Which one?"

Her phone chimed to tell her she had a message, and she had to force herself to pay attention to Darryl's answer.

It can wait. In fact, the more she thought about it, the more she decided Wes *should* have to wait. He'd used her to make Sophie jealous—even get back with her, as it turned out—and then he'd played with her emotions, sending her mixed signals and a flirty text. She wasn't just a fill-in replacement until he got back together with his ex. She had a life—was working on getting one, anyway.

After another hour of talking, Darryl walked her to her car. "Good night," he said with a nod.

"Night."

He turned away, took a couple of steps, and abruptly turned back. "I was going to play it cool, but I'm just gonna go ahead and ask you to dinner. And I'm hoping we can do it soon."

She waited for the excitement, a flutter—something. Maybe she just needed to get to know him better. "I'd like that."

He grinned and she noticed a dimple in one of his cheeks. He was totally good looking and wasn't playing games. The potential for a relationship was definitely there.

Her phone vibrated in her purse, "SexyBack" filling the air again. This time she didn't waste a moment before silencing it. Darryl asked her if Sunday was too soon for dinner, and she told him it was perfect.

She got into her car, dug out her phone, and listened to the voice mail Wes had left.

"Just bored and wanted to say hi. Got a show in a little bit. Same venue. The crowd will probably request the sexy female singer we had last time we played."

Dani was about to call him back—she could tell him about her date and ask if he'd booked his flight for the retreat yet—but she hesitated, wanting to hold on to this hopeful moment, where Darryl had potential and the evening held promise of more nights getting to know him. If she heard Wes's voice, she'd start questioning everything between them, like she had been all week. She didn't even know what to do about the "sexy female singer" comment he'd made. He'd never called her sexy before.

Her stomach twisted. All the walls she'd thrown up to keep herself from overanalyzing everything with Wes were crumbling down. She was thinking of that kiss at the wedding and how a simple brush of his fingers had set her skin on fire.

Maybe the key to moving on was distancing herself from Wes. Not all the way. Just a little bit.

Enough to let someone else in.

• • •

Wes slid his phone back in his pocket, wondering if Dani were avoiding him. She hadn't called all week, and now she wasn't answering his calls. He sat down and ran a hand through his hair.

"You okay, man?" Paul asked, busying himself with his guitar.

Not sure. "Yep."

Paul leaned his guitar against the wall, then came over and sat next to him. "You talk to Dani recently?"

Tension coiled through his muscles, from his neck to the tips of his fingers.

Paul nodded. "I figured that was it. If I would've known, I wouldn't have hit on her the other night."

"I've told you before, I don't… She's just…" He slumped forward and ran a hand over his face. No use hiding it now. "It doesn't matter. She lives in Arkansas."

"Yeah, that part blows." When Wes shot him a *No shit* look, Paul shrugged. "Just saying." He picked up his guitar and started strumming it.

Wes sat back in the ratty recliner. It looked more and more like he should call Sophie and see if there were still something there. He just wasn't sure he was ready to completely give up on Dani yet. He kept telling himself he'd wait and see what happened when he flew out there. That everything would become clear. But it was getting muddier and he was feeling pathetic.

She's just busy with work so she can land that promotion. A promotion I'll help her get so she can live far, far away from me.

It did blow, but that didn't change the facts. Time to let this—whatever it was—go.

And there was one way to ensure he followed through... Wes took out his phone and finally made the call he'd kept chickening out of all week.

Her voice held a note of surprise when she answered.

"Sophie? I need to talk to you. Can we meet?"

Wes tossed back the disgusting, warmed-over-way-too-many-times coffee and put the chipped mug in the office sink. His boss had called him in early, and after last night's concert, he was hovering in that half-awake/half-asleep stage.

As disgusting as it was, the coffee worked its magic, bringing his muscles and brain cells back to life. Unfortunately, the thinking started right away. Dani never called last night, and he'd made a plan to meet up with Sophie right after work today.

It gave him plenty of time to cancel, which was good, because now he was thinking it was a stupid idea. His footsteps echoed across the room as he paced. Where was Gerald? He needed to get this meeting over with and get up in the air. He was booked for helicopter tours all day, which was good because it meant getting paid, but bad because it meant no trick flying, instead giving all the facts about the city he'd recited a hundred times.

He shouldn't complain, though. It was still better than any other job, and he'd feel better once he was airborne. Thoughts were easier a couple thousand feet in the air.

Gerald walked into the office, smoothing his comb-over with one hand. "Hey, Wes. Let me just grab a cup of coffee and we'll go into my office."

Minutes later, Wes was seated across from his boss, a sinking feeling in his gut.

What if he's not happy with me? I really do love this job. It's no adventure tours, but—

"I'll get right down to business. I've been thinking about retiring for a while, but I wanted my business to keep on going, and now I think I've found someone who could be successful at it." Gerald leaned forward, elbows propped on his desk. "You're a great pilot, and you've got a good head on your shoulders."

Realization sounded bells in Wes's head, and he straightened. "Are you saying you want me to...?" He couldn't even bring himself to finish, in case he'd misunderstood.

Gerald nodded. "We'd work out a transition. You'd get a bump in pay as you took over some of my responsibilities, I'd show you the ropes, and in a year, it'd be yours. Somewhere along the way we can try some of those adventure tours you were asking about. See how they do." For a moment, Wes could only stare, his body buzzing as the idea sunk in. His own company. More exciting tours. A pay increase. Basically, it was his dream on a silver platter. He scratched his head. "What about Ed? He's been here longer than I have."

Gerald jutted out his chin and nodded. "True. But his

social skills are shit and I don't think he's got a lick of business sense in his head. He's a good pilot, but not fit for running my company. You'd rather work for Ed?"

"No. Not at all… It sounds great. And I've been looking at the other routes we can fly. We could do a stopover with water skiing. Or rock climbing—I've got lots of ideas. But what about the loans? I'm not sure I can afford to buy you out, even in a year."

Gerald tossed a folder at him. "That's what the year plan looks like. Take some time and see what you think, then let me know."

Wes lifted the file. He opened it, but the words and figures swam together. He needed to talk to someone about this, and Dani was the first person who popped into his head. He wanted to tell her the news. Ask her what she thought. Maybe even see if she could help him out with the marketing if he did follow through. Especially if he were going to add some exciting tours to his schedule.

"We can discuss more details later, but I wanted to put it out there as soon as possible," Gerald added.

"Thanks. I'll look it over and let you know." Wes reached across the desk and shook Gerald's hand. He had to refrain from skipping out of the office.

Praying she picked up this time, Wes dialed Dani. He swore when it went to voice mail. "Hey, I've got some big news, and I really need to talk to you. Call me back ASAP."

By the time Wes sat at the restaurant, waiting to meet Sophie, Dani still hadn't called him back. He fought the urge to be the crazy possessive boyfriend who left her dozens of texts and messages—especially since he wasn't even her boyfriend. But damn, she was just going to ignore him from now on? If that were the case, he should've gone for it the night before she left—at least he would've had one unbelievable night with her that he could hold on to, even if they could never be like that again. Why hadn't he told her how amazing he thought she was, taken her into his bedroom, peeled off that purple dress, and kissed every inch of her skin like he'd wanted to?

Heat wound through his body and his breaths grew shallow. He took a large drink from the glass of cold water in front of him and exhaled. Those thoughts weren't ones he should be entertaining while waiting for his ex-fiancée to show up.

What the hell was I thinking?

"Wes?"

His stomach clenched. He took another deep breath and stood. "Sophie. Hey."

Her hair was pulled back, her features as pretty as ever. Months of awkwardness were crammed into the space between them. He almost went for a hug but ended up simply pulling out the chair opposite him. She settled into it, and he pushed it forward.

He sat back down and rubbed his palms on his jeans. He hadn't expected his nerves to be bouncing all over the place. "How've you been?"

Sophie ran her fingers along the edge of the table. "All right."

Silence.

Wes took a couple of gulps of water, wishing it were something stronger.

"I talked to Audrey yesterday," Sophie continued. "She joked that she's decided to move to Hawaii, so I guess that means she's enjoying her honeymoon."

Wes didn't want to think about his sister on her honeymoon. How could conversation be so hard when he and Sophie used to spend more time together than not, talking about everything and nothing? Hell, they'd been planning a life together.

He leaned forward, crossing his forearms on the table. Dani wasn't answering the phone and he was dying to tell someone his news. "I might be getting a promotion at my job. More than a promotion, really—I might be running my own business in about a year."

"That's great, Wes."

He told her his plan to add a few adventure tours. She listened politely but kept her mouth clamped, her expression not giving away anything. "So, what do you think?" he asked.

"Are you sure you want to fly helicopters for the rest of your life?"

"Who's ever sure about anything?"

She closed her eyes, and when she opened them, they were glossy. "I'm sure I made a mistake, and now I'm too late. I thought maybe if I could make you jealous… If I could just get you to fight for me at all, then I could accept everything else…" She lifted the napkin and dabbed at her eyes, the white fabric coming away with black smudges. "Did you call me here to talk about business? Is that why you wanted to see me?"

He picked up his fork and tapped it against the table to give his hands something to do. "No. Not really." But he should be able to talk about the business if their lives were going to be intertwined again. The question was, did he really want that? Time to think logically. He lived here. He'd just gotten offered his dream job. Dani lived almost a thousand miles away. What chance did he have of being with her the way he wanted to when she didn't even answer his calls?

And the girl he'd once loved so much he'd asked her to marry him—for real, not just for pretend—was sitting across from him and possibly still loved him. She said she'd made a mistake. He'd never heard her admit that before. And if he were reading her right, she was saying that showing up at the bar with that guy was to get a reaction from him instead of trying to hurt him. Was everything that happened today fate? Was it telling him to give things with Sophie another chance?

Or was he settling?

He plunked the fork back down. "Actually, I wanted to talk to you about something else. I wanted to talk about us."

"Us?" she squeaked.

Now was the time to admit his and Dani's engagement was nothing more than a sham.

If he wanted to give it another go...

Sophie placed her hand over his. Their eyes met and he thought, *What do I have to lose?*

• • •

Dani stared at the e-mail with the agenda for the retreat and room assignments.

NEWLY ENGAGED COUPLE DANI AND WES ARE IN THE ROSE CABIN.

After reading that, she'd clicked on the link to the website of the place where they were staying. The mini cabins were joined all in a row, doors facing out, each one decorated in different themes. And there was another theme going on— no couches. Just a big bed in the middle of the room and a dresser off to the side. She didn't want Wes to have to stay on the floor, but she didn't think she could handle sleeping in the same bed.

Wes had called earlier, too. A knot formed in her gut. She felt guilty for ignoring him all week, and she supposed it was time to call him back. She'd had her space and had gone on two more dates with Darryl. They had a lot in common, and he was a total gentleman. There was real potential there. So she should be totally fine talking to Wes now.

Just friends.

She listened to his voice mail, the guilt increasing when he asked her to call him back ASAP, then hit the button to call him. For something she'd done a hundred times, it was crazy how foreign it suddenly felt. Her heart was in her throat and her mouth had gone dry.

By the fourth ring she didn't think she'd even be able to talk.

His recorded voice played, telling her to leave a message. She was about to tell him she couldn't wait to hear his news. Then it hit her that his big news was probably about Sophie. What if they were re-engaged?

Her heart stopped as that thought took hold.

Engaged or not, though, he wouldn't back out of the retreat, because he felt obligated to help her like he said he would.

Sophie'll hate that.

Good, she thought, a thrill going through her. But then she remembered how hurt Wes was when Sophie dumped him. How he'd asked Dani to help make his ex jealous at the wedding.

It was probably even why he'd kissed her like that onstage. Her lips burned with the memory. She could smell his cologne, feel his arms wrapped so tightly around her, the residual heat traveling through her body.

For show. It was all fake, Dani. Why didn't her heart get it? *Stupid confused heart.*

She opened and closed her mouth, trying to figure out if she should leave a message, but then Linda from sales stepped into her cubicle. Dani hung up and twisted to face her.

"So excited to hear you're engaged now!" Linda leaned against the gray wall. "And Norah says he's a helicopter pilot."

Dani figured it was too late to get herself out of the lie, so she nodded. "Yep."

"I can't wait to meet him at the retreat. I just knew you'd find someone. So, show me the ring!"

Dani lifted her bare hand. "I, uh, forgot to wear it today."

Linda's brow furrowed. "Forgot?"

"It's all so new and I was in a hurry this morning, so..." The truth was she'd shoved the ring away, not wanting to look at it. Not to mention she'd been on a couple of dates this week. Dani kept the fake smile plastered on her face until Linda left, then dropped her head on her desk. What a mess. Admittedly it was nice that all the women in the office were beaming at her instead of giving her you-poor-spinster-you looks.

Bet those looks would be even more pity-filled when she told everyone her engagement had fallen through. She lifted her head and looked at her phone, wondering if she should call Wes back and tell him to just forget about the retreat altogether.

Chapter Thirteen

Wes headed straight to his bedroom. He was so exhausted his eyelids were drooping, and he had to be at work early again tomorrow. He shucked off his clothes and stumbled into bed, trying to figure out if he'd made a mistake tonight.

Maybe he was an idiot. But he had to believe it was the way to go right now, even if it ended up screwing him over later.

Now he needed to figure out what to do about the offer to take over the company.

His phone rang. "My Life Would Suck Without You" meant Dani—he'd changed it after her performance at the club. Over the past few days, he realized how well it fit.

She'd called while he'd been out with Sophie but hadn't left a message. He rolled over, grabbed his jeans off the floor, and dug through the pocket for his phone. For a moment, he considered saying something sarcastic as soon as he answered, about how it was such a relief she was still breathing and knew how to dial. But he was too happy to hear her voice, and he was dying to tell her about his job offer.

"Did I wake you up?" she asked, her words rushed together. "I know it's late."

"I wasn't asleep yet. And you know you can call me whenever." He turned onto his side, resting his head on his arm. "So, you'll never guess what happened today."

"You broke your ankle doing something stupid."

All the bitterness he'd felt toward her for ignoring him this past week melted. "Close. I might do something stupid, and there's always a possibility of ankle breakage. Especially if I get my way."

"Okay, I think I'm way off, then."

"So guess again."

"Just tell me."

"I'll give you a hint. It's something to do with my job."

"Are you going to get to do your Indiana Jones adventure tours?" she asked.

"It's sounding like a real possibility. Can't call it that, of course."

"'Cause that would be crazy."

"More like copyright infringement," he said. "So you need to help me figure out a name with all your mad marketing skills. But that's not even all of it…" He told her about the possibility of taking over the entire company. "It'd probably be hectic and stressful for a few years, but then it would be mine, and I could do some different tours. I'm trying to think logically, but it's hard when everything inside of me is screaming to go for it."

She was quiet for a couple of seconds, and he held his breath, waiting for her to tell him it was a crazy idea. That finally he'd gone too far for even her to indulge his ideas, which meant his family would totally freak.

"Wow. That's… That's huge, Wes. I'm so happy for you!"

The excitement in her voice made him sit up. "So you think I should do it?"

"Well of course you've got to look at the financial side before diving in—if you want, I know a good accountant who can help you go over all the ins and outs. But it sounds perfect for you, it really does."

"I think it might be." He thought of the helicopters in the hangar at work. They could all be his. His to maintain. To fuel. To freak out over if they weren't full of people, making money. He leaned back against the headboard. "It'd be more responsibility than I've ever had, though. I can't just walk away if I get a new idea. Not this time. And what if I end up driving the entire company into the ground?"

"If it's what you want, you'll find a way to make it a success."

Come run it with me, he wanted to say.

"You know, I was thinking earlier today how both of our lives are so crazy right now—yours even more so with all the good news about your job—and maybe this retreat's at a bad time. Work's going really well and I'm sure I can land this promotion, even if I don't get much time to talk with the boss, so you don't have to come out here." It was like she'd taken up speed talking and it took him a couple of seconds to process it all.

"It's not a problem. I already bought the plane ticket."

"I'm sure they'll let you change it. Having you pose as my fiancé for this thing was a stupid idea in the first place."

Everything inside him turned from warm and happy to cold and confused. "But the retreat will be a good chance to take some time off before life gets crazy. And you know I'd never give up a chance to be outdoors, competing, forcing you to do dangerous things with me."

The line was dead quiet, and frustration was creeping in. He needed another chance to be with Dani. To see if he'd made the right decision tonight.

"If you're sure…" she finally said.

"I am. I'll see you Wednesday night. It'll be fun, Dani. And don't worry. I'll behave myself." He thought of all the excuses he'd have to hold her hand. Maybe even steal a kiss. Or ten. "For the most part."

She laughed, and like always, the sound made him smile. It made him wish he were there to see her eyes light up, her lips curve. "Well, when you put it like that...I'll see you then. And congratulations again on the new job."

"You're next," he automatically said, but realized that meant she'd still be way too far away.

He set his phone on the nightstand and lay back again, thinking about this roller coaster of a day. So many ups and downs. At dinner, he'd been so close to giving a relationship with Sophie another try.

Then Dani had called. He'd wanted to answer—but Sophie was eyeing him, and he knew that wasn't the way to start over with her.

Sophie had slipped her hand off his and straightened. "I don't know what I was thinking, coming here. Just tell me one thing, Wes. I want to know—I need to know—if you started sleeping with Dani before we broke up. Please just be honest, because it's killing me."

Wes clenched his jaw. "If you knew me at all, you wouldn't have to ask."

"That's not fair. You were always on the phone with her. You went to visit for a week and then a few months later, you end up engaged. What am I supposed to think?" Ever since he and Sophie had broken up, he'd focused on everything great about her. But he'd forgotten that there were fights that *didn't* include his friendship with Dani. She always called his hobbies immature, told him he needed a "grownup" job, and apologized to her family for his jokes.

"Nothing was going on with Dani before you dumped me, Soph." He was about to admit he still wasn't involved with Dani, but he realized that would be a lie. There was something inside pulling him to her, and distance or not, he had to try. Better to crash and burn than to forever wonder.

"I'm sorry I asked you here," he said to Sophie. "I thought… I guess I thought we needed resolution. But I think I'm just making it worse. So I'm sorry you and I didn't work out, I'm sorry if I hurt you, and I wish you the best."

Sophie stared at him for a few seconds, then dropped her chin. "Yeah. You, too."

Not sure whether he'd later regret his choice, he'd paid the bill and left. He drove around the city for a long time before coming home. And now that he was thinking about it, he realized that in a way, Dani was responsible for not just his and Sophie's relationship failing, but all his failed relationships. Not only because no one could believe they were just friends, but also because he knew there had to be more girls like her out there.

But there weren't. Not exactly like her, and she was who he wanted. So he was going to that retreat with her, he'd be the best damn fiancé ever, and at the end of it, he'd lay it all on the line and hope if they were good enough friends, they'd survive it, even if she didn't feel the same way.

What he really hoped would happen, though, was that she'd tell him she felt exactly the same way.

Chapter Fourteen

Just in the nick of time.

Dani made a copy of the signed contract and then walked into Bill's office and tossed it on his desk. "The account's ours." Hopefully it would be *hers* once she got the promotion. "I've got to go pick up my fr—fiancé—at the airport, so I'll see you tomorrow."

Bill nodded. No *good job*, no friendly *good-bye*. No *thanks for working your ass off this week and talking our new client into signing a contract.*

When I'm in charge, she thought, *I'm going to be much cooler to the people who work with me.*

Dani stopped by her cubicle, shut down her computer, and grabbed her purse. A mixture of excitement and apprehension swirled through her stomach, leaving it tingly and cramped at the same time.

Because of her confused emotions over Wes, she'd worried his being at the retreat with her was a bad idea. But with so much on the line, she was glad he'd insisted on coming. She'd be calmer, he was a total charmer, and everything would be okay. The next three days would include lots of "team building" activities, and if she had her way, lots of chatting up the boss and proving she deserved a promotion.

All she had to do was focus on her goals. Rock the retreat, land the promotion so she could help out her family financially and they could all breathe easier, and continue to get her life back, which may or may not include Darryl. He hadn't called for a few days, but she hadn't called him, either—she was enough of a mess without adding any new, maybe-kinda relationships into the mix.

Dani got in her car, fired up the engine, and gave herself a mini pep talk.

I'll be fine. Wes and I are friends. I've just got to keep my feelings in check.

Or, in other words, she just had to hold back.

• • •

The lights of Little Rock grew brighter, buildings and freeway lanes starting to take shape. Flights he wasn't in charge of piloting weren't nearly as fun, but at least he was that much closer to Dani.

He tapped his fingers on his bouncing knee, and the man next to him scowled. Wes almost wanted to tell him it was okay—he wasn't nervous, just in love. With his best friend.

His heart squeezed. He'd been determined to cross into more, but he hadn't realized until now how true the love part was. This wasn't like a normal dating situation, where he was getting to know the other person a little at a time. He already knew her. Already loved her. And now he was in the kind of so-crazy-he-couldn't-think-about-anything-else love.

It felt reckless and dangerous, the same feeling he got whenever he was about to cliff dive or do a stunt in his helicopter. Frantic energy coursed through his veins; his knee bounced higher.

The airport took shape, and then the wheels were down, bumping against the asphalt. The landing was a little rough, and he couldn't help thinking *his* landings were much smoother. All the passengers sprang into action as soon as the FASTEN SEATBELT sign dinged and shut off.

Wes ran a hand across his jaw. He still wasn't quite used to it being so smooth; his face still felt naked without his scruff. Small price to pay if he got to kiss Dani, though.

Finally it was his turn to grab his bag from the bin and exit the airplane.

He spotted her right away, even though she looked different than she usually did. Her hair was down and straighter than usual, and she was wearing tight black slacks and a crisp white button down. He'd never seen her dressed so all-business before. Her gaze moved down the line of people, getting closer and closer. Then her eyes met his, and his heart skipped a beat.

He crossed the distance between them in a few quick strides and hugged her. It was like hugging a wooden post— her arms stayed down by her sides and her body was stiff. Then she was stepping back. Her eyes followed the movements of people around them, not meeting his.

Why's she all cagey and closed off?

She scuffed the floor with the toe of her shoe. "How was the flight?"

"Would've been better if I got to fly the plane."

That got him a half smile. "I'm surprised they managed to get it off the ground without you."

"Me, too."

Her shoulders lowered, the tension slowly draining from her body. "I'm surprised. I figured you'd be about back to the mountain man look." She reached up like she was going to smooth a hand down his face but then dropped her arm last minute. "Anyway, you ready?"

He hiked the strap of his duffel bag higher on his shoulder and stepped toward her.

She took a large step back and spun around.

This was the furthest thing from the scenario of this moment he'd cooked up in his head. If only he knew what was going on in *her* head. He didn't want to make a mess of things before the retreat—if she didn't feel the same way about him, it'd be a whole lot of awkward over the next four days. So he'd take it slow, even though everything in him revolted at that thought. All the time together would be the perfect opportunity to show her how great they were together.This time, he was all in. No more holding back.

• • •

Dani gave Wes the tour of her apartment, which didn't take long, since it was just the living room and kitchen, bathroom and bedroom down the hall. "I already pulled out the blanket and pillow," she said, pointing to the pile next to the couch. "Watch TV if you want. My kitchen doesn't have much food, but you're welcome to anything in there."

"You're going to bed already?" Wes asked.

Yes, otherwise I might accidentally throw myself at you. Hopefully it'd be easier to control herself at the retreat. She'd be in work mode, not thinking about how they were alone and how he looked with his shirt off and—

"Dani?"

She gave her head a little shake, trying to rid it of that image. "We have to get up early tomorrow and you know I suck at that. I have to be awake enough to drive the hour and a half it takes to get there."

"I'll drive." Wes grabbed her hand and pulled her toward the couch. "Stay up for a bit with me."

"But you don't know the way."

"There's this amazing thing called GPS that tells you exactly how to get there." He gave another tug and she moved toward him.

"But you never listen to the GPS because you think you can figure out a better way."

"My way's always more fun." He pulled her again and their bodies were almost touching.

Dani tried to swallow but a permanent lump was in her throat. As much as she'd told herself to hold back—that she could control her attraction—it wasn't really working. Not now that she could feel the heat coming off him and his eyes were on hers.

Space. She needed space. She sat down on the end of the couch, leaning her back against the armrest and pulling her legs up to create a barrier.

Wes sat on the other end. Two creases formed between his eyebrows and she worried he'd noticed she was acting weird. They'd always had such a natural ease, one no one else understood, and she wished it hadn't disappeared with that kiss at the wedding.

"So?" he asked. "Anything new happen in the last few weeks?"

"Well, it's not anything yet really, but I did go on a couple of dates with a guy."

Wes sat back, his lips pressed in a tight line. "No offense, but you do tend to pick losers, so I'm going to save you a few months and say you should just get rid of him now."

"Hey," Dani said, kicking her foot against his thigh. "Okay, so maybe I've picked a *few* losers, but that doesn't mean I'm incapable of finding a good guy. Besides, I… Don't make fun of me, but I started a membership through an online dating site, so technically I didn't pick him, the site did. I've been out with him twice, and he's nice."

"Ah, *nice*. Sounds thrilling."

"And he plays basketball."

"The key to any good relationship."

The more he mocked her, the more flustered she got. *Not all guys can be like you*, she bit back. Desperate to change the subject, she said, "What about the job offer? You take it yet?"

"Not officially. I'm still looking over some things. I did find a spot for white water rafting. Just need to get the certification."

"So you can save all the people you convince to do crazy things?"

"Pretty much." He patted her foot. "You're freezing again. Here." He shifted, tucking both her feet under his leg. "I actually brought the files. I was hoping one night we'd have some time to go over it all. I'd love to get your opinion before I sign away my life."

"Sure," she said, and then silence stretched between them. For background noise, she punched on the TV, settling on ESPN.

Wes hooked his arm over her knee, leaning toward the TV. "Five bucks the Cardinals come from behind and win this game."

"You're on," she said, and he grinned. "Would now be a good time to tell you that Johnson got hurt yesterday and isn't playing?"

His smile faded. "Really? Damn." He rubbed his fingers along his jaw and shrugged. "Oh well. I'm standing by my bet."

"Prepare to lose, then." After a few minutes, she let her head fall back. Exhaustion seeped into every muscle, every bone. Her eyes drifted closed as the game played in the background.

There was something so cozy and secure about Wes and the noise and the fact her feet were now warm underneath his legs. As she drifted off, she had the hazy thought that this was all she'd need to be happy for the rest of her life.

Chapter Fifteen

Wes glared at the GPS when it told him to "Turn right in point two miles." Like he couldn't see the sign. He shouldn't feel so bitter at an electronic voice telling him what to do, but it was driving him crazy.

He glanced at Dani. Her seat was reclined, her eyes closed, a completely peaceful look on her face. He punched off the GPS. She'd never know, and now he could relax and drive. He still wasn't sure what to make of how closed off she'd been last night. He'd promised himself he wasn't going to hold back, but it was stupid to ruin everything if she clearly didn't feel the same way.

He took a sip of his now-cold coffee, swearing when it sloshed out of the cup, over his thumb and onto his shirt and pants. He looked up in time to see the shift in the road and all the orange barrels set in place to keep traffic out. He merged behind a semi, following it onto the rough pavement.

The bumps and loud noise the tires made hitting the road didn't even faze Dani.

When, a good hour later, he realized he was on the wrong

road and had been for quite some time, he started hoping she would stay asleep for the entire drive. No such luck. Of *course* that was the moment she started stirring. She squinted at the clock, rubbed her eyes, and looked at it again, scooting forward. "Aren't we there yet?"

Wes grimaced. "Small problem."

She whipped her head toward him. "Wes, tell me you followed the directions on the GPS."

"There was road construction and we got a little off, but we're back on track now. This will save us time, anyway. There was only one lane and they were stopping traffic for miles."

Her eyes moved to the tiny gravel road and then to the blank screen of the GPS. "You turned it off?" He flinched at her high-pitched shriek. "I have to be there for my presentation, Wes. This isn't *roam the backwoods of Arkansas* adventure time."

"But if you were going to roam the backwoods, what better way to do it than with yours truly?" He flashed her a big, goofy smile.

She clenched her jaw and he could practically see the steam coming out of her ears. Okay, so joking hadn't worked, which meant she was really pissed. "Look, I'm sorry. I shouldn't have turned it off, but I'm trying to fix it. Just a few more turns and we're there. We'll still be on time." *Close to it, anyway.* He reached over to pat her knee and she jerked away.

"Do you even know where we are?" Before he could answer that, she was punching on the GPS. "This is just like when we went up that trail in the mountains on four wheelers and ran out of gas. I told you over and over that we should turn back, but *nooo*, you knew a shorter path."

"Well, we've got plenty of gas," he said, and she shot him a dirty look that, honestly, was pretty scary, though he'd never admit it out loud. If he thought he could say anything right, he'd try it, but he figured the best thing he could do was get them there as fast as possible.

She shook her head and pulled out her cell phone. "I don't understand how it's so hard to just leave on the GPS so you know where to turn. And I think construction is preferable to being in the middle of nowhere"—she held up her phone—"with no freaking service."

The GPS started repeating, "You have veered off course," over and over. "See," he said. "It's obnoxious. And bossy. And it's not even working."

"It works when you first turn off the road." She punched a few buttons and it started recalibrating the route. "Why can't you just go the way you're supposed to?"

"Why can't you just relax and enjoy the adventure?" he shot back before he remembered he was supposed to be in apology mode. Shit, he was screwing everything up. Being lost was frustrating for him, too, though. Once she cooled off, he'd apologize again and get things back on track. He just needed to get her to her presentation first.

A loud *pop* sounded and the car swerved. Wes had to fight the wheel for control. The car skidded to the side of the road, spitting out dirt and rocks behind them. He depressed the brake, easing them to a stop the best he could with a definitely flat tire.

"*This* adventure?" She flung off her seat belt and pushed out of the car.

With a sigh, he followed her. He rounded the trunk and looked at the shredded black rubber that remained where a full tire should have been. Dani had her arms crossed and was muttering something in Spanish.

Well, this wasn't going to win him many points. Right now, he wasn't feeling all warm and cuddly about her anyway.

After changing the tire to the dinky donut spare, one he

couldn't drive very fast on, they took off again, the mood in the car arctic. By the time they pulled up to the Masterpiece Lodge, they'd spent forty-five minutes in tense silence.

"Great," Dani said. "Everyone's already gathered outside, staring at us, and we've got to pretend to be an engaged couple who just can't wait to get married."

Usually she went along with whatever—she was his go-to for an adventure, after all—but now she was acting like being late was practically the apocalypse. This was the kind of thing Sophie would be pissed about.

"They'll understand that we got a flat tire," he tried, doing his best to keep calm, hoping it'd rub off on her.

"No, they'll see that I wasn't there when I needed to be. No one gives a shit why. It'll end up listed as the reason I didn't get the promotion—like *I'm* the one who can't be counted on." She shot him a searing glare, her implication that *he* was the one who couldn't be counted on clear.

"You need to relax."

The fire in her eyes made it obvious that was the wrong thing to say. "Relax? You know, we can't all be like you, Wes. So carefree about everything. Getting a company dropped in your lap. One that basically lets you fly around and go on adventures, like you'd be doing even if they *didn't* pay you. So don't even act like you understand."

"It's not my fault you don't like your job—"

"You don't get it." She shook her head and the exasperation in her voice made her words come out clipped. "You've never had to try to support your family on top of everything else. You don't know what it's like to need a job so badly it keeps you up at night. You're just a spoiled boy who's never had to grow up." She charged out of the car, slamming the door loudly enough for it to hurt his ears.

In all their years as friends, they'd never fought—argued or disagreed, sure, but not like this. Anger burned through him. Spoiled? Never grew up? That was what she thought of him? Well, she was a tight-ass who freaked out over stupid things.

Her co-workers were staring, and now he was supposed to go out and pretend he was happy to be around Dani. He never would've guessed it'd be hard to play her fiancé, even before he'd thought there was more to their relationship. He took a deep breath and slowly exhaled, then got out of the car, fake smile plastered on his face.

He grabbed Dani's hand, squeezing hard enough that the diamond on the ring jabbed into his palm.

"Danielle," one of the smarmy-looking dudes said. "So nice of you to finally join us. I was starting to wonder if I'd have to do the presentation myself."

Wes's bitterness toward Dani shifted to the prick who was calling her out in front of everyone. "It's my fault we're late. Apparently I'm one of those people who gets lost even with GPS. And is also unlucky enough to have a flat tire."

"You must be Wes," a woman said, stepping forward and extending a hand. "We've heard so much about you."

"Yes, this is my fiancé," Dani said. She introduced him to the group. The prick's name was Bill, and all their past phone calls about the guy she worked with clicked into place. If Wes had anything to say about it, this guy was going down.

Dani glanced around. "Did Wayne already go over the schedule?"

Bill grinned, a cocky smile that Wes wanted to smack off his face. "He did the welcome and said he was looking forward to the presentations." He glanced at his watch. "You might want to have your fiancé check you into your room so we can go set up. We're the first presentation, and that gives us about ten."

Dani glanced at Wes.

"I'm on it," he said.

"It'll be under my name." She ran a hand through her hair and he noticed the tension in her shoulders. It'd been so many years since they were in college, he'd forgotten how stressed she used to get before their class presentations. She always accused him of relying on his "charming personality" while she busted her ass.

He leaned in close. "Hey, you got this. Don't let the jerk throw you off."

She stared up at him, and as much as the words she'd said to him earlier stung, he wanted nothing more than for her to go nail her presentation. She opened her mouth, but Bill broke in.

"Time's a wasting," he said.

She hiked her laptop bag up on her shoulder and took off with him. Wes headed to the front desk, second-guessing what exactly he wanted with Dani. If she'd never see him as anything more than a slacker who didn't care about his job, then she must not believe in him the way he believed in her.

• • •

As she stood in front of the room filled with her boss and colleagues, Dani's stomach churned, her palms got clammy, and heat rose to her face and stayed there. That wasn't unusual for her, but the hollowness in her chest over the fight with Wes was.

She couldn't believe she'd said such awful things. She was still thinking about it when Wayne Bridges told her and Bill to "Go ahead and get started."

Maybe it was the boots, giant belt buckle, and cowboy hat, but her boss's appearance made her feel like she had eight seconds to ride to success or get trampled by bulls.

But the thought of bull riding made her think of how she and Wes had rode the mechanical one at Whiskey River. She pictured him tipping his imaginary hat at her with that grin and some of the tension filling her body eased.

Okay, I can do this. Focus on the facts, the way Wes had me do in the helicopter.

It cleared her head, but unfortunately, it didn't stop Bill from constantly stepping in front of her during the presentation, talking over her when she started to make a point. Blocking every move she made. If he were a defender in a basketball game, she'd plow right over him. She should. But every time she'd glance at Wayne, her confidence would waver. As a result, Bill looked like he was the one who'd done most of the work.

She should care more—a distant part of her did. But she kept glancing out the window at the stupid tiny tire on her car, wondering if she'd just destroyed her friendship with Wes because of it.

I can't lose Wes. He's one of the best things in my life.

"Very impressive," Wayne said when Bill wrapped it up, showing off their high success rate on new accounts. "You work this as a team?"

"I take point, of course," Bill said.

Bastard. What she wanted to say was, *And I do all the work,* but she knew it'd just come across as bitchy, and she'd been that plenty today already. She couldn't stand there and let it look like she didn't do anything, though—not when her happiness and bank account were relying on not working under Bill.

Finally, she found her voice, even if it did come out shaky. "I work with the customers and the ad design team. Bill and I started integrating the method two months ago and already we've seen an increase in sales on every project we've attacked with it."

Wayne nodded. She thought he was going to ask her some questions. She braced herself, remembering that she knew her work backward and forward and could answer anything he threw her way.

But he simply called up the design team for their presentation.

The meeting was only an hour, but it dragged. All she'd wanted to do the entire time was find Wes and apologize. But once it ended and she was finally free, she couldn't seem to force her feet to move over to him. He was surrounded by company wives and was already hamming it up.

Wes broke away from them and walked up to her. "How'd the presentation go?"

"Not sure. I don't think I made a very good impact. I'm just not that good at being in front of a room full of people, especially when one of them is my boss."

"I'm sure you did fine. And you've still got time to impress everyone."

"I guess," she said. All she had to do now was apologize. Maybe she should ask him to duck inside the room.

But then all her female co-workers were closing in, wanting to be introduced to Wes and talk wedding details. At least she and Wes had already made up their story so they didn't have to do it on the spot.

Dani felt like a fraud the whole time, but she was already too deep into the lie to do anything about it. Wes played his part like a champ, too, even though he probably regretted his decision to come to Arkansas.

Finally, the crowd cleared. Dani glanced at Wes. He tensed, no longer keeping up the happy, in-love front. Standing right next to him, thick silence hanging in the air, she felt further away from him than she did when two states stood between them.

Her heart gave a painful squeeze. "Do you hate me?"

Wes dropped his head, the longer wavy pieces of hair falling over his eyes. "I just didn't realize that's how you see me."

"I don't, though. Your spontaneity and carefree attitude are the things I love most about you." There was a weird beat after she realized she'd used the word *love*, but she powered through. "Sometimes I wish I could be like that, but then reality hits. I know what it's like to grow up without money for clothes or food. It's why I worked my butt off to get basketball scholarships—I knew that was the only way I'd get to go to college, and even then my family had to sacrifice a lot to help me out. And now I worry I got the wrong degree, so it was all just a waste, and I'm..." She ran a hand through her hair. "I'm just so stressed trying to get this promotion."

"I'll admit that I don't know about having to take care of my family, but it doesn't mean I haven't ever struggled with money or other things. One of the reasons my family has that house is because my father passed away and left it to my parents, and trust me, we'd rather have him around still. And it's not like they bail me out or pay my bills. *I* pay for my stuff with money *I* earn."

She flinched at his harsh tone and how underneath it, she could still sense the hurt her words had caused him. "I know. That was unfair of me to say, and I'm really sorry."

He gave one sharp nod. "I'm sorry you're so stressed about the promotion."

"It's not just that." She twisted to him, her chest achy and raw. "My abuela's health is slipping, and my mom can't afford the medical bills that keep piling up. I've been trying to help, but with my own expenses... It's not enough."

Wes's expression softened. "Why didn't you tell me? If you need money—"

"I don't want money from you."

He frowned. "Why won't you let me help? You take care of everyone else, but you never let anyone take care of you."

She crossed her arms. "I don't need anyone to take care

of me."

He grabbed her wrist, pulling it loose. "I know. But I want to." He looked down at her and then drew her to him, wrapping his arms around her. "Just please let me know if there's a way I can help."

She swallowed the lump in her throat, nodded, and then hugged him back.

"We cool now?"

"Super cool," she said with a smile, stealing one of the phrases he always used to say in college. Out of the corner of her eye, she saw Bill talking with Wayne and sighed. "If I can get the promotion, I'll be able to take care of myself. But of course Bill's over there chatting it up with the boss, probably convincing him I should be under him forever."

Wes looked over at them, then back at her. "It's okay. I have a secret weapon." He slid his hand down her arm and clasped her fingers, tugging her toward her car. He took the keys out of his pocket, opened the trunk, and lifted out the basketball she kept inside.

Dani stared at the orange ball. "I'm starting to doubt you know what a secret weapon is."

"Well, technically, *you're* the secret weapon."

She shook her head. "And it keeps getting worse and worse."

Wes tossed the ball in the air and caught it. "Hey, it's either this or singing. Need me to find a microphone?" He tossed the ball again, and she swiped it out of the air.

"What did you have in mind?"

Chapter Sixteen

Five minutes later, Wes and Dani stood across from Bill and some guy named Joe, who was apparently one of the design guys. Buzzing energy zipped through Wes's limbs, the way it always did before he and Dani worked their magic on the court. Her boss was seated at a nearby table in the shade, talking to a few of her co-workers. Other people were milling around, not paying much attention to the basketball court.

Hopefully that would change soon.

"Care to make the game a little more interesting?" Wes dribbled the ball a couple of times, then threw it at Dani.

She let it smack her palms and then frowned as she watched it bounce away. "My bad. I'll get it."

Man, he loved this part.

"I was thinking," he continued loudly, making it seem like he was trying to get their attention on him so they didn't notice his partner struggling to get her hands on the ball. After years, they could usually gauge just how "crappy" she needed to be. "We should make a friendly bet. What do you say? Twenty bucks?"

Dani picked up the ball and came over, dribbling high and sloppy.

"Twenty's fine," Bill said, condescension and smugness dripping from the words. "I'd go higher, but that's hardly fair, what with…" He glanced at Dani.

"Are we making bets?" Dani said. "The usual fifty?"

Wes bit back a smile. "I wasn't sure if Bill and Joe would be up for fifty." Reeling them in, and…

Joe and Bill exchanged a quick glance and a nod. "Fifty's fine for us," Bill said.

Aaaand they'd bought it, hook, line, and sinker.

He tossed them the ball. "Game on, then."

As they played, Wes would glance at Dani's boss now and then. He, along with everyone else in the area, was now honed in on the game, watching as she sunk shot after shot. Bill was pretty good, but out of shape, and Joe was obviously not a baller. Bill's face got redder and redder the longer the game went on, the veins sticking out.

"I'll get her," Bill yelled, pushing Joe toward Wes.

Wes dribbled down the court. He pulled back for a second and then drove right, faked a shot, and passed underneath the hoop, where Dani now was, nice and open.

She shot.

Nothing but net.

And that was game. Dani flashed him a wide smile. Whether or not her boss was impressed, at least she'd enjoyed showing up the prick she worked with.

As they were getting water and toweling off, her boss came up to them. "Wow, that was some game. I didn't know you played."

"She was on her college team," Wes said, knowing Dani wouldn't brag herself up enough. "I'm just lucky I get to play with her instead of against her."

"It was quite impressive," Dani's boss said to her, and

then introduced himself to Wes before returning his attention to her. "I've been meaning to talk to you about the new marketing strategy. How much of that is your doing?"

Wes nudged her when she didn't immediately answer.

"It was my original idea…" Her voice was a little shaky, and he silently urged her to put more certainty in her words. She lifted her chin, and he could see the confidence seeping in. "Bill and I do work on things together, though I do most of the mockups and the interfacing with the customer, and I pride myself on being good at that."

"That's what I thought. I like that you didn't throw him under the bus, though." Wayne nodded. "Very impressive. The basketball *and* the new strategy. I look forward to seeing what else you can do," he said, then walked away.

Dani turned to Wes, eyes wide. "Did that just happen?" Before he could answer, she threw her arms around him.

He hugged her back, lifting her off her feet for a moment and then setting her back down.

His gaze moved to her lips. He could get away with kissing her, right? He was her fiancé after all.

Someone cleared his throat. Bill. Add it as another reason Wes wanted to punch him.

"Are you two going to do the boat races?"

Dani slid her arm around his waist. "We'll be there."

"My wife and I will be, too. Care to make a bet? Double or nothing?"

Dani glanced at Wes and he nodded. "You're on," she said.

Bill smiled like she'd told him he won the lottery. "I guess now would be the time to tell you I was on the rowing team in college, and my wife's a fitness instructor." Another smile and then he walked off.

"So our new goal is to beat that guy at pretty much everything, right?" Wes asked.

A competitive gleam hit Dani's eye. "Oh yeah. He's so going down."

. . .

By the time Dani and Wes made it back to their very floral room, she was soaking wet and her muscles were burning. "Now *that* was fun."

The race had been close, but she and Wes had edged ahead of Bill and his wife at the last minute. Wes decided the best way to celebrate was to tackle her and send them both overboard.

"If the ball game didn't do it, your boss will for sure remember you now. Maybe a little more for the way your wet shirt is clinging to you than your work ethic..." His eyes ran down to her plastered-on shirt.

She shoved him. "Thanks a lot."

Speaking of leaving little to the imagination, his shirt was shaped to him, reminding her exactly how fit he was. She could even see a hint of his dark tattoo through the light fabric. She wanted to run her fingers up it, across his chest, down his abs... The temperature in the room shot up and her breaths came faster and faster. Even though she knew they were in too different places in their lives to make a relationship work right now, the friends with benefits for a night or two seemed like a better and better idea.

Of course, that was still complicated. Not only the awkwardness it might cause, but because he was in love with someone else. Lead filled her lungs. She swiped her wet hair behind her ear and twisted the ends around her finger. "By the way, did you ever talk to Sophie? About what I told you?"

For someone who couldn't be with him, her heart was sure hammering hard, panic rising over the possibility that he was back with her.

"How is that 'by the way'?"

Was he purposely avoiding the subject? Did that mean things between him and Sophie were good or bad? "I just meant to mention it earlier but forgot. You know, due to our day starting out all shitty-like."

"Am I ever going to live that down?"

"If I let it go, you'll just get us lost on the way back."

"I'll probably do that anyway," he said with a grin.

She stuck her tongue out at him. Really, she was glad they could joke about the fight. If they were dancing around it, she'd know it was still between them. "Okay, so back to Sophie."

He crossed his arms, and she tried not to notice the way it made the muscles in his chest and forearms stand out. "She and I talked, but I realized it's just not going to work with us."

Excitement and hope zipped through her—she barely restrained herself from jumping up and down. Trying to be considerate, in case he was hurt about it, she clamped back the smile trying to break free and said, "Oh. Sorry."

"I think she actually did me a favor by dumping me. We would've had problems down the road, and in the end, we didn't want the same things." His eyes locked onto hers. "You thought I should go back to her? You wouldn't have cared?"

Working at nonchalance, Dani shrugged. "If it would've made you happy, I could've dealt with it. But if it's not what you want…" She shrugged again—apparently her shoulders were all twitchy today.

He was still staring at her, though, like he was waiting for something. She didn't know what, so she decided to get back to the business at hand. "Before I forget, I realized today that talking about how you're taking over a company in North Carolina might be bad, seeing as how they're not going to want to give me a promotion if they think I'll move."

"I might not be taking over."

"Oh, right, we still need to look at the financial aspect. We'll do that later."

"Even then. It might not be what I want, either."

Dani didn't know why she was surprised. Maybe her words this morning about his impulsivity had been too harsh, but obviously she wasn't completely wrong. And if he couldn't stick to a career doing something he loved, she was glad she hadn't deluded herself into thinking he could stick with one girl forever.

• • •

Dani hadn't even flinched this afternoon when he'd asked how she would feel about him getting back together with Sophie. After the mess this morning and her mentioning the guy she'd recently started dating and— Seriously? She didn't even want to tell him she was glad he wasn't with Sophie because it'd be easier for their friendship? Obviously he'd deluded himself into thinking there was something more between them.

As they headed toward the tables for dinner, he put his hand on her back. He wanted to show everyone she was his, even if it was only for show. His pulse thudded in his fingertips, in every spot where he touched her. She was wearing this super sexy black skirt that showed off her legs, too, and he couldn't stop staring at them. Staring at all of her.

She'd said she needed to look nice for dinner to make sure she continued impressing her boss. Clearly she cared about this job, and if she was here and he was in North Carolina, there was no chance of a relationship. So now he was thinking of looking for job opportunities here, which was crazy if she was just going to be dating some dude a website hooked her up with.

He normally jumped right in, thinking he'd figure out the

rest later. But if he were thinking about changing his career—moving to Arkansas, which, okay, he really didn't want to do—then maybe it was time for him to slow down and use his head.

It would be easier if he could think straight.

They settled at a table with several of her co-workers. "Oh, before I forget…" Dani leaned in and put her hand on his thigh, her breath hitting his neck.

Definitely not helping the think-with-his-head thing. Which was probably why he turned his face to hers and softly kissed her lips. "Yeah, babe?"

Her eyebrows twitched higher and her lips parted. Glancing down, she swiped that one strand of hair behind her ear. As usual, it simply fell forward again—he loved that she never stopped trying, though.

"I…I forgot what I was going to say," she added.

The woman across from them beamed. He couldn't remember her name, just that she was the administrative assistant. "Oh, aren't you two sweet. I remember when my George and I were engaged. I was much younger than you, fresh out of high school. But I just knew after we went to prom that he was the one for me." She took a sip of her water. "So how did you meet?"

Dani licked her lips and he had to restrain himself from kissing them again. "We were both history majors in college."

"So you've been dating since college? I thought this just happened. Weren't you with that other fellow for a long time?"

Gotta love people with no filter. This lady was obviously one of them.

"Well this"—Dani gestured between herself and him—"did just happen. We've been friends since college, though."

He slid his arm over the back of her chair. "She's been my best friend for years. It's kind of stupid I didn't figure it out earlier."

Dani glanced at him again. Her cheeks were pink and she fidgeted with her fork.

"And when exactly did you figure it out?" the woman asked. "How did you know she was the one?"

Dani's eyes met his, and he stared back at her, wondering which story to tell. Fact or fiction? "It kind of snuck up on me, honestly. She was my best friend, and then one day... Well, I missed her when she was gone. I couldn't stop thinking about her. Finally I realized the girl of my dreams had been right in front of me for years."

He rubbed circles on her back. "She was a little hesitant at first, I think. But no one can say no to this face for long." He grinned at the woman and she smiled right back. Well, he'd won one girl over. He returned his attention to Dani, continuing to rub her back, trying to see if he was anywhere close to making it two.

. . .

Dani was having trouble breathing. All the things Wes had said were how she'd felt after the wedding, and this was only screwing her up more. She didn't know when they were acting and when things were real. But the way her heart knotted told her it didn't care whether a relationship between them was logical or not.

And that kiss. It was short, but there was still something to it. She wanted to forget her co-workers were surrounding them, wrap her arms around Wes, and kiss him with reckless abandon.

Linda asked where they were getting married, though, and then she was telling her about the museum and answering questions about the wedding, throwing out whatever popped into her head. The other people around them chimed in, talking about their own weddings and offering her and Wes wedding and marriage advice.

After dinner, they even got some "words of wisdom" from Mrs. Bridges. Wayne chimed in, and Dani was able to relax and have an easy conversation with him. So even though her heart was confused, the plan she and Wes had come up with was working.

But what would the cost be when they were done? She couldn't help but wonder if it would be worth it if she could never be in a relationship again without wishing it were Wes instead.

By the end of the night, the basketball game and boat race and her overanalyzing every move Wes made were catching up to her. She was tired and her head was spinning, and she couldn't wait to get away from the crowd.

As they walked back to their room, Wes took her hand, lacing his fingers with hers. Intoxicating warmth spread through her veins, and she couldn't help but lean into him a bit.

When they got to their cabin, she reluctantly pulled her hand free to get out her room key. Once the door was closed behind them, they stood in the entryway staring at each other, neither of them making a move farther inside.

It was this strange, unsure ground she'd never stood on with him before. Was it her imagination or was he acting nervous, too?

"Tonight with that whole conversation about how you knew I was the one, and the attentive fiancé bit..." She swallowed, but her heart had lodged in her throat. "You're a better actor than I expected."

He put his hands on either side of her on the wall and leaned in. "Actually, I'm not that good of an actor."

Her pulse hammered in her ears. "So you're saying we should practice a little more? Maybe, say, start with the kissing part?" She couldn't believe she'd said it. Every second felt like an endless, terrifying eternity as she waited for him to blow it off as a joke or back away.

But he moved closer, closer...until their lips met, and everything inside her unraveled. He pressed into her, their hips bumping together. Every inch from knee to shoulders connected, all fire. His hands moved to her face, pulling her closer, deepening the kiss.

His weight on her, his tongue in her mouth, exploring hers. She welcomed the burn, the dizziness, craving more and more. Rational thoughts were trying to poke through, telling her this was a bad, bad idea.

"I don't think—" she started.

"Don't think." He moved his mouth to her neck and sucked lightly on it.

If he hadn't been pinning her to the door, she would've fallen to the ground. He ran his hand up her thigh, then pulled it over his leg. He continued to trail kisses up her neck, across to her jaw, back to her mouth. His fingers slid under her skirt, up her hip, hooking the string of her underwear.

She gasped, then took over the kissing, biting gently at his bottom lip. He groaned and pushed into her harder. Her heart jolted and desire flooded every inch of her. Yes, there was a whole lot of lust going on, but it was more than that. She was in love with Wes. The thought terrified her a little, but it didn't keep it from being true. He knew her better than anyone else in the world and still accepted her. He was the guy she could spend hours and hours with and never get sick of.

He was the one setting her body ablaze in ways she'd never experienced before.

She slid her hands under his shirt, smiling against his lips when she felt his muscles twitch under her touch.

"Dani," he half whispered, half groaned. Then he yanked

her to him and stroked her tongue with his until her knees were weak and she could no longer tell where she ended and he began.

She gripped his shirt and started to pull up, wanting to see and feel more of him. All of him.

The knock on the door made her jump. She froze, feeling like she was caught doing something she really shouldn't do.

But damn, did she want to.

The knocking came again. "Dani, hun?" *Linda.* For all her talk about knowing what it was like to be engaged and in love, she sure needed a reminder of what people in that stage did the moment the door was closed.

"Just ignore it," Wes whispered.

"Then they'll think we're in here having sex," she whispered back.

He nodded in a way she took to mean, *Well, yeah.*

Dani exhaled a shaky breath, working to make her voice normal. "One second," she called out, then tugged down her skirt and ran a hand through her hair. She glanced at Wes again, his eyes lit with passion, and everything inside her turned to mush. He was right. She should've ignored it. Too late now, though.

Wes dropped his forehead onto the wall next to the door. She cracked it open, blocking him and peering out at Linda. George was by her side.

"We noticed your other tire is flat as we were walking by your car," Linda said. "If you need help, George can help you."

Wes grabbed the door and swung it open a couple more inches. "Thanks so much for letting us know. I'll take care of it tomorrow morning, first thing."

"Thanks. And good night." Dani waved at them, watching until they were two dark outlines. A moment ago, all she wanted was for them to leave so she and Wes could get back to what they were about to do. Without him running his hands over her, though, rational thought was creeping in, along with a sobering dose of reality. Yes, she was in love with him—she thought her heart might burst from how much she loved him—but this whole situation was beyond complicated.

It was times like this she cursed herself for always having to think things through. She closed the door and put some space between her and Wes. "About what just happened."

He took a step toward her. "Nothing happened quite yet." His deep voice and the promise of satisfaction behind his words sent her pulse racing again. She swallowed and took another step back. More space. She needed more space. "Wes…" She didn't even know what to say. Here he was, her best friend, and they'd been kissing and their bodies had been… Warmth pooled low in her stomach—man, it was hard to focus right now.

Wes held up his hands, like she was going to scare if he made too many quick movements. Maybe she was. "Okay. We'll slow it down."

"It? Are we…? I mean, this can't…" She put a hand to her forehead. "We're going to mess it all up."

"Or it could be great."

She shook her head, and for some reason, tears were springing to her eyes. "Trust me, I've thought about it a lot, and it won't work."

A crooked half smile hit his lips. "You've thought about it? For how long?"

"Pretty much since I landed in Charlotte. But especially after the wedding, when you kissed me." She lifted her eyes to his. "Why'd you kiss me?"

"Same reason I did in college. I wanted to see what it was like. Maybe back then we weren't ready. But I'm ready now, Dani."

She shook her head. "I don't think things through enough

when I'm with you. It's like my common sense goes out the window."

"Common sense is overrated, anyway."

She had to pull out the reason that caused her the most pain to speak aloud. "We live in different states."

"That's not set in stone. You could move in with me. Or I could move here. We'd figure everything out. Let's just talk about it."

Her head was already trying to shut it down, but a glimmer of hope rose up—she couldn't help but want to figure out a way to make it work. "Fine. Talk. Which means you need to go over there." She pointed at the chair. "I'm going to stand over here. And spare me the comments about how hard you are to resist."

He grinned. No comment needed.

The textured wall was unforgiving on her hip. Good. It'd keep her mind sharp and focused. "The thing is, I know you too well. You always jump in and expect it to all work out. But this is different. I need this job promotion and you're preparing to take over an entire company. The timing's not right."

"I'm willing to look at job options here if that's what it takes."

Her heart soared, and she was instantly thinking of him being in Arkansas with her. Coming home to him after a hard day at work. But her momentary happiness deflated when she thought of him trying to make do with an office job he'd hate. "I won't let you give up a once in a lifetime opportunity for me."

"And you're not willing to consider the possibility of moving back to North Carolina?"

She thought about not having a job and relying on Wes not only for herself but to help support Mama and Abuela. That would be enough to ruin a relationship before it even started. In time, maybe she could save up. Look for jobs that might take her back to North Carolina.

She exhaled. "Maybe eventually. Until then, though, I think it's best we don't put pressure on ourselves either way. If it's meant to be, it'll work out. If not… Well, you'll always be my best friend and I *need* you as that, especially right now." Her chest ached at the truthfulness of the words. She didn't want them to be true, but she'd thought about this way too much in the last few weeks.

He leaned his elbows on his knees and dropped his head in his hands.

"You know I'm right," she said. "Even though I'm sure that right now you're thinking of how to prove me wrong."

"I know you well enough to know that once you set your mind to something, it's almost impossible to change it. Once in a while a dare will work, though."

"It's not going to work now."

His blue eyes lifted and cut right through her. "You took a chance on moving out here with Steve. Why him and not me?"

"That was a mistake, obviously." And maybe it was the reason she was too worried to try it again. Steve had left her with an expensive rent to pay by herself, and not that she'd expected financial help with her surgery, but she'd expected him not to leave her alone to recover. What if she moved her entire life and then Wes changed his mind about her in a month? Or even a year?

Wes's jaw clenched. "But you were still willing to risk it." He stood, the tension in the set of his shoulders clear. "I'm going to go change that tire now."

"Wes." She stepped into his path as he moved for the door. "Wes." All that kept coming out was his name, because she didn't know what else to say. Hot tears sprang to her eyes. "Please don't go now. We're not done talking this out."

"There's not much point in talking anymore. You've made that perfectly clear."

The cool air wafted into the room as he swung the door open, and then it was just her alone in the room, the echo of the door slam reverberating in her ears.

• • •

Wes stepped into the cool air, but it didn't help the hot anger pumping through his veins. How could this night go from the best ever to the worst so quickly? He'd had Dani right there in his arms. He'd thought nothing had felt so right in his entire life.

And then it'd all come undone so quickly.

Honestly, it'd kill him to give up his dream job. He'd actually considered it, though. But Dani...

Her refusal to even try was a punch to the gut, deflated lungs, a slap in the face. The girl he'd always loved in one way or another not only thought he was irresponsible, she thought he wasn't worth the risk.

The front tire of Dani's car was totally flat. So maybe she had a point about him not thinking things through. Who expects a back road to be full of nails, though? You'd think no one would ever drive them.

Maybe that's why no one did.

Since he knew she didn't have another spare tire, it wasn't like he could even fix it. He sank down on the curb in front of the car. He didn't know how he was supposed to go back and sleep in the same one-bed room as her or manage to be all cheery and "we're engaged" tomorrow in front of her co-workers. His first instinct to wait until the end of the trip had been a good one, but like Dani said, he was impulsive.

Damn Linda and George. If they hadn't interrupted, he and Dani wouldn't have slowed down so she could start overthinking everything like she always did. He might even be lying next to her right now, nothing between them.

He shook his head. This wasn't helping. But damn, he was frustrated as hell. In every way possible.

His phone rang, vibrating in his pocket. He dug it out and glanced at the display.

A conversation with Mom—especially if she mentioned the wedding—would probably make him feel worse. It was hard to ignore her call, though. He always felt like she'd know that he could've taken it but didn't.

He sighed and answered.

Sobs greeted him first.

His nerve endings pricked up, and he sat straighter. "Mom?"

"It's A-Audrey. She's in t-the hospital."

Chapter Seventeen

Wes burst through the door. One look at the grim expression on his pale face told her something major was wrong. Dani shot to her feet. "Are you okay?"

"Audrey's in the hospital. My mom doesn't know how bad it is and she's freaking out. I told her I'd be there as soon as I could." He grabbed the clothes he had lying around and shoved them into his suitcase.

"By the time you drive to Little Rock, there probably won't be any flights out until tomorrow."

"I'll just drive all the way home, then."

"In what? My car's got a flat tire and a dinky spare."

"I'll figure something out," he said, and his harsh tone made her flinch. Under normal circumstances that might be enough to scare her off, but not when she could see the pain hanging heavy on his features.

She placed her hand on his arm. "Wes. We'll get you there first thing tomorrow."

He closed his eyes and dragged a shaky hand through his hair. "I'm the one who told her to go have an adventure.

I even teased her about being boring. So she and Matthew went cliff diving. And now—" His voice cracked. "What if she…"

"She won't." Dani wrapped her arms around Wes's waist, hugging him tightly. "It'll be okay."

For a moment, his body remained stiff, but then he relaxed, his weight nearly making her stumble. She maneuvered them over to the bed and sat him down. He looked lost, and she didn't know how to fix it or what to say. So she bent down and pulled off his shoes, then urged him to lie down. His gaze remained on the ceiling, unfocused.

Dani's mind started whirring, all the ways to get him back to North Carolina as soon as possible flashing through her mind. Get tires and then her car? Taxi to the airport? *I should go book him a flight.*

She was about to get online, regardless of the spotty Wi-Fi, but Wes caught her hand. His eyes met hers, and there was so much vulnerability there it ripped her heart in two. So she crawled onto the bed next to him.

They didn't talk. Didn't move.

Just lay there in silence until Wes's breathing slowed and his body relaxed.

Dani waited a few more minutes and then carefully propped herself on her elbow and looked at him. Her heart swelled and a giant lump formed in her throat. Again, she thought of how much she loved him—everything about him. His sense of humor, his kindness, and even his impulsive nature and how he challenged her. She loved the slope of his nose and his wavy hair and his strong jawline, clean-shaven or covered in stubble. She loved him so much it sent a pang of longing through her, yet she'd rejected him earlier tonight.

I must be stupid. All the analyzing in the world didn't matter if you couldn't imagine not spending every day next to someone. Here she was, clinging to a job she barely liked.

Would she even like it more if she got promoted?

Not enough to give up the one steady thing in her life. When she'd been listing off all their obstacles and reasons they couldn't be together, she'd somehow forgotten that. No matter how impulsive he was, he'd always been there for her. Maybe they'd crash and burn, but Wes was right. It was worse not to have taken a chance. And he deserved for her to take that chance on him.

She needed to make everything up to him. She figured getting him back to his family as soon as possible was a good place to start. Keeping her movements slow, she got off the bed and tiptoed to her laptop. After several searches she managed to book him a flight to Charlotte. There was only one ticket, so she wasn't sure if she should try to get a later flight or wait and see what he found out when he got home—she didn't even know if Audrey and Matthew were in Charlotte, or if they were still on their honeymoon.

Now do I try to get my tires fixed first thing in the morning so I can drive him or ask a co-worker to borrow a car?

She glanced at Wes's sleeping figure and hoped with all her heart that his sister was okay. She knew he'd never fully recover if she weren't.

"Are you sure I can't drive you?" Dani asked.

Wes shook his head. "I want you to stay here and get that job you deserve."

"I don't care about that. If you need me, I want to be with you."

He came over and put his hand on her shoulder. "You did enough. Thanks for taking care of the flight."

She didn't know what else to say, so she just nodded.

"And about last night…" He rubbed the back of his neck.

Dani waited, her breath caught in her throat, thinking of sleeping next to him all night.

"You were right," he said. "A romantic relationship would be a bad idea. I'm glad one of us was thinking clearly."

Pain. So much pain pushing against her chest she couldn't breathe. Regret and all the things she should've said filled her, deepening the ache. But she held them in, too scared to say them now.

A yellow cab pulled up outside.

"Call me when you know more, okay?" she said.

"I will." Wes cupped her cheek. "Take care of yourself. And good luck on that promotion. I have a feeling it's already yours."

Dani bit her lip to fight the tears threatening to spill.

He gave her a quick, one-armed hug and then he was out the door and heaving his suitcase into the taxi.

She wanted to burst out the door yelling, "Wait, I made a mistake!" Instead, she watched the car pull away, the red lights cutting through the gray morning.

So she told herself it was for the best.

But the hollow aching between her ribs spoke much louder.

• • •

By the time Wes got to the hospital in Mooresville, he was exhausted. Last night he'd nearly had a meltdown, but he'd held his feelings in check all day, and they were scraping at his insides, wanting to spill out.

He swallowed them down. Mom would need him to be strong, so he'd be strong. All he knew now was that Audrey and Matthew had decided to do something crazy their last week off before work, and taking Wes's suggestion, had driven the thirty minutes to Mooresville to go cliff diving.

The hospital was small, so it didn't take him long to find Mom in the waiting room. Her eyes were red-rimmed and puffy. She threw her arms around him and cried on his shoulder, and for a moment, his heart broke as he thought the worst must've happened—that his sister was gone.

"She's still in the ICU, but her vitals look better." Mom sniffed. "You just missed Jill. She went to grab some food."

"How's Matthew doing?"

"He's a wreck."

Now Wes wished he hadn't asked. It didn't help anything. For about the hundredth time today he wished he would've taken Dani up on her offer to fly back with him. He needed space from her, though. Last night when she'd hugged him, he'd almost forgotten that she'd crushed him only minutes before.

Almost.

He could see how hard she was trying this morning to make it up to him, like her not loving him enough could be fixed by plane tickets and hugs.

"Is Dani coming?" Mom asked, as if she could read his thoughts.

"She had to work." Wes glanced down the hallway. "I want to see Audrey."

The halls of the hospital were all white, with lights that emphasized their blankness. The scent of disinfectant saturated the air, and he tried not to think about the fact that the cleaner might've been used to clean up blood.

When they reached the ICU area, Dad embraced him and patted his back. He tried to say something, but all that came out were a few indecipherable words and tears.

Wes peered through the window at Audrey. Machines surrounded her, flashing stats. The peek of her face he could see was puffy and bruised. His little sister. Broken.

What if they never got to talk and laugh together again?

Right now he'd even take her yelling at him, telling him he'd stolen her thunder.

What if she couldn't walk again?

Never woke up again?

Tears lodged in his throat. The walls were closing in; his hands were trembling.

He turned to Matthew, fighting the urge to ask how he could let that happen to her. But his eyes were bloodshot, his face blotchy. It was as though all the life had been drained out of him and a shell of a person was standing there instead.

And suddenly he was glad that he and Dani hadn't crossed into more. If anything happened to her, he'd still be crushed, but the thought of being that invested in another person made his insides grow cold and hard. From now on, no more relationships. No more acting on impulse, either. It had gotten him rejected by his best friend and dealing with a sister in the hospital in critical condition.

He was done with his stupid adventures.

With everything.

Chapter Eighteen

Dani spent half her day explaining why Wes wasn't there. And then her co-workers would ask the inevitable question: Is his sister going to be okay?

And she didn't know.

At lunchtime, Bill drove her into town in his truck to get two new tires, even offering to put them on. It made her feel kind of guilty. Maybe he wasn't as awful as she'd thought. Or maybe he was feeling guilty, too.

Finally they had a grand good-bye, all *Go team* and *Let's make the rest of this year even better than the last!*

As soon as people scattered, Dani took out her phone and calculated the time again. Wes should've landed more than two hours ago. She hated to bug him, but she was dying to know how Audrey was. How he was.

She bit her thumbnail, telling herself to give him time.

Then she called him anyway.

No answer.

It took her thirty minutes to pack up and clear out. She turned on her GPS, following the instructions to the letter. So boring. So opposite of Wes. As mad as she'd been that he'd gotten them semi-lost, she'd take it now.

She tortured herself by replaying their kiss last night—his hand sliding up her leg, Wes asking her to move to North Carolina, the fight afterward, sleeping in the same bed. Over and over on shuffle.

By the time she got home, he still hadn't called. She scrolled through her contacts and paused on Kathleen's name. She'd insisted they exchange numbers for wedding planning purposes. Her finger hovered over the contact name. Would it be bad to call his mom?

Oh, who cared? She *had* to know what was going on.

It rang twice and then Kathleen answered.

"I'm so sorry to bother you, but I was wondering how Audrey was doing."

"She's breathing and they say her heart rate's steady," Kathleen said.

In the background, she heard someone say, "Yeah, when they talk to us in that bullshit way that makes me not believe half of it." That voice—it was Wes. Just hearing him made her pulse stutter. He was there. Not calling her. And she'd called his mom.

"Is he okay?" Dani asked.

There was a couple seconds' pause. "I'm not sure. You wanna talk to him?"

"Yeah."

Sounds of shuffling and muffled voices came over the phone. "It's Dani."

"…don't want to talk to her."

"She's worried about you. Go on. Let your fiancée know what's going on."

"She's not my fiancée." His voice was no longer muffled but loud and way too clear. "Dani and I aren't engaged, okay? I just told you we were so you'd leave me alone. But we're not getting married. In fact, I'm not getting married. Ever. So now you know."

She'd never heard him sound so cold before. Kathleen came back on the phone. "Dani?"

"Can you please hand me over to Wes? Tell him it's important."

More shuffling noises.

"What?" Wes asked into the phone, his harsh tone slicing into her. Oh, if he wanted to fight, she'd give him a fight.

"I can't believe you just said that. It's one thing to fess up, but you really couldn't think of a better time to tell her than right now, when she's worried about Audrey?"

"You're the one who called her."

"What the hell's wrong with you?" She clenched her jaw, working to tamp down her anger. "Last night...and this morning. I thought we were okay."

"We're fine. I just need a break. If you actually care about Audrey, you can call my mom and have her update you."

The call cut off. He'd hung up on her.

Dani stared at the screen of her phone in shock, his words slowly sinking in. *A break? He needs a break from me?*

She slammed her phone down on the kitchen counter so hard the case popped off. The anger heating her veins faded bit by bit, leaving her cold. Sorrow took over as everything inside her unraveled, one thread at a time.

Tears pooled in her eyes. For so long she'd held them back, but now she let them flow. She was sick of having to be the strong one. The rational one. The one who worried all the time about bills and money and the damn healthcare system. She wanted to be the one who went out, got drunk, met some hot dude, and brought him home for the night, no care for what happened after.

Actually, that was a lie. She didn't want the empty one-night stand. She wanted to finally be in a relationship with

someone who loved her and understood her and would wrap
his arms around her and tell her it'd all be okay.

And maybe she'd had a shot at that and she'd blown it.

Now he was gone.

And she was alone, crying.

Worried she'd ruined the best thing in her life.

Over the next week, Dani's co-workers kept asking her how
Wes's sister was doing. She'd thought about calling his mom
to find out, since Dani was giving Wes his stupid break, but
thanks to their fake engagement, his mom probably hated her
now.

So she just told them Audrey was recovering, hoping
it was true. She was tempted to send a mass e-mail telling
everyone she wasn't engaged anymore, but the boss still had
the promotion hanging over their heads, keeping them in
line. No doubt he wouldn't think an emotional mess who just
got dumped would be a prime candidate for the job.

First thing Friday morning, Wayne called her into his
office. Her stomach sank as she walked past the gray cubicles,
the office she'd lusted after for so long, to the corner room
with a view of the entire downtown.

Wayne turned his chair to face her and gestured toward
the cushy leather seat across from his desk. "Have a seat."

Dani sat, back straight, feet firmly on the floor. She knew
Mark, one of the other junior execs up for the promotion,
had just been in, which meant this was the meeting to tell her
she was still assigned to work under Bill. For the rest of her
life. Mediocre pay, all the work and none of the credit. He'd
probably even tell her that she lacked the marketing degree,
but if she kept working hard, she'd eventually be able to move
up.

All bullshit.

For the hundredth time, she wished she'd decided to move back to North Carolina with Wes. Who cared if she couldn't pay her bills and had to eat ramen for life?

But then there were her mom and grandma to worry about. At least Abuela had gotten the go-ahead earlier this week to be taken off oxygen and was doing better. Mama had even sounded rested when Dani talked to her last night. It was almost enough to give her hope they'd make it yet.

"I was very impressed with you at the retreat," Wayne said. "I've looked over all of the projects you worked on for the last year, and I'm very happy with the progress you've made." He leaned forward, and she waited for the "but."

"I'm offering you the position of senior executive," he said and her heart started pounding. She'd dreamed of those words for so long, she almost pinched herself to make sure it was real. "We're expanding, and I'd like to put five people under you. I'd hold you accountable for your clients and theirs. It means more hours, more responsibility, and more accountability. Do you think you can handle that?"

"Yes, sir," she automatically said, even though her head was swimming at the thought of the added stress. She could do it, though. She was good under pressure.

"Good. I think this is going to be a lucrative move for the entire company." He extended a file toward her. "Here's the contract."

Dani took it, working to keep her hands from shaking. It was such a big moment, and the mixture of excitement and a pinch of fear was making her slightly dizzy. She opened the file and glanced inside. The annual pay made her heart skip several beats—it was more than she'd expected. She skimmed down the page, reading all the stipulations, and then her heart stopped for a different reason. "Two years?"

"That's standard here. If you break any of the codes

of conduct or we're unhappy with your work, we maintain the right to end the contract, but we'll be putting a lot of work into your training and your department. We ask for a commitment of two years."

The words *two years* played through her head on a repeating loop. In two years, Wes would probably have his business up and running.

He might have a new girlfriend. A new fiancée.

Her stomach turned to stone; breathing became difficult.

But if it was meant to be, it was meant to be, right? And maybe the promotion was just what she needed to enjoy her job more. Yeah, that sounded likely, what with all the long hours and accountability and seeing the outside world she never got to hang out in from her fancy new office window.

Now she couldn't breathe at all.

"Dani?"

She whipped up her head. "I'm so honored. I just… Can I take a little time to think it over?"

His bushy eyebrows drew together and his mustache twitched.

"I mean to read the contract. I feel like I'll miss something, and I like to be thorough. I'll do the same with the accounts I work on, I assure you."

The chair gave a small squeak as he sat back in it. "Sure thing. Why don't we meet back up at the end of the day. About six?"

Six? As in he expected her answer today? Shit.

"Sure." She flashed him a smile she hoped looked less fake than it felt and left his office, practically sprinting back to her desk.

Her eyes ran over the text in the contract again, stopping on the two years.

It was stupid to think about throwing away that big of a salary for an adventure junkie guy who might change his mind about her tomorrow, right? Hell, he'd already changed his mind about her.

But he didn't know how she felt. Because she'd never told him.

She drummed her fingers on the top of the desk. She'd e-mailed him two days ago. Just a simple *hey, hope you're okay* e-mail that asked about Audrey.

Desperately hoping he'd e-mailed her back—at least that'd mean he was ready for their friendship break to be over—she opened her inbox.

There were some work e-mails. More junk from dating sites. One from the site she actually paid for. One from the guy said dating site claimed was a perfect match for her. She'd been avoiding Darryl as much as Wes had avoided her.

She started composing a new e-mail to Wes with the subject line URGENT!!!! Because apparently she'd now started using all caps and multiple exclamation points, too. She'd been so worried crossing the friends line with Wes would destroy what they had that she'd never thought about what blocking her feelings could do to her. She started pouring them out in the message.

But then she decided it was pathetic and deleted the entire thing instead of sending it.

She stared at the contract for a couple more minutes. She even picked up a pen, determined to sign her name. But then she saw Wes in her mind. Scruffy, clean shaven, five years ago, now. Laughing. Broken after hearing about his sister. Asleep next to her. At home in a helicopter.

Wes, Wes, Wes.

She was so in love with him she could hardly think straight anymore. He was on her mind as soon as she woke up in the morning, all throughout the day, when she tried to fall asleep at night. She knew she'd never love another guy as much as she loved him. A giant lump lodged in her throat.

She took out her cell phone and scrolled to his name. She was already on the verge of tears, so she wasn't sure if her heart could take him ignoring her call.

To dial or not to dial. To sign or not to sign. She needed to talk to him. Needed to do something.

Before it was too late.

• • •

"It's too late," Wes said to Audrey. Apparently Mom had filled her in on the fake engagement, but that didn't stop her from pressing the issue now that she was not only awake but also able to sit up and eat semi-solid food.

He blamed the fact that she was all sickly for why he'd spilled his guts on the fake engagement, from acting like he loved Dani to somehow realizing he did.

Audrey winced as she scooted up in bed, and he reached over and readjusted the pillow for her. "I can't believe you lost her," she said.

"Were you even listening to me?" Wes sat back and ran a hand through his hair. "She was never mine."

"You forget that I met her when you two really were just friends. When you showed up at home, announcing you were engaged, I didn't believe it at first. But then I saw the way you two watched each other when you thought no one was looking. That's when I realized what you never had with Sophie. I knew you wouldn't get bored with Dani."

"She thinks I'm impulsive and irresponsible."

"You are."

"Gee, thanks." He shoved her yogurt toward her. "Eat more."

"The Wes Turner I know doesn't give up that easily."

"Which is why I keep telling you to eat."

"You know that's not what I mean."

Wes sighed. "Maybe someday Dani and I will figure it out. But it's not a good time. I don't even know if I want my job anymore."

"That's such bull," Audrey said. "You can't stop doing what you do because I got scared last minute and fell into the rocks instead of jumping into the water."

For the first few days it was touch and go, but even now that she was awake and could eat semi-solid foods, it wasn't like she'd be able to leave the hospital any time soon. "But you punctured a lung and you're going to have to get screws put into your leg."

"Yeah. Thanks for the reminder." Audrey put her hand on his arm and locked eyes with him. "I don't blame you for my accident. Don't use me as an excuse to stop doing what you love. And you shouldn't make excuses for not being with the person you love, either."

"Hey, I tried. It's not up to me."

"Really? Aren't you the one ignoring her calls? Her e-mails?"

"Fine. I'll e-mail her back."

"Don't be a wuss. You owe her a call." Audrey held up her hand when he tried to talk. "Don't give me that 'I need a break' crap. You need *her*, Wes. You're a mess without her. Have you told her that?"

"I don't see the point."

"You think it makes you weak. That Matthew being out there, pacing the halls and crying makes him weak."

"I didn't say that," Wes said.

"But you thought it. He's worried because he loves me, but I know I don't have to worry because he'll be right by my side the whole time, surgeries, rehab—whatever. We'll get through it together. Having someone like that doesn't make you weak; it makes you strong."

"Fine. I'll call." He patted his pocket and frowned. The

last time he'd used his phone…Mom had called, asking him to grab some breakfast for them and he'd…put it in the cup holder. "I left it in my car. I'll call her later."

He started to sit back down but Audrey scowled at him. "So go get it and call. Then come back here and tell me what happened."

"I'm not gonna—"

"Look what I have to watch on TV. Look at it!" Audrey pointed at the tiny image that showed some kind of soap opera. "I prefer real-life drama. So come back here after you call. And sneak me in a Diet Coke, 'kay? I need something more than yogurt and this mushy oatmeal."

Wes rolled his eyes but left the room knowing he'd end up coming back. At least to deliver her a soda—he owed her that much. On the elevator ride down, he wondered if he really could go back to flying a helicopter and planning extreme adventures. What if people he took got hurt? He didn't want to be responsible for that.

Wes hung his head. Maybe he *was* afraid of responsibilities. Afraid of running a company and screwing up a business one of his favorite people in the world had built from the ground up.

The elevator doors popped open with a *bing* and the dingy stale air of the parking garage filled his lungs. For the past week, this had been his outside time, and honestly he was starting to miss the outdoors. Being the person flying through the skies at two hundred miles per hour.

He grabbed his phone and turned it on. His muscles tensed when he saw he had a voice mail from Dani. Would it be good? Bad? A *stop ignoring me, you asshole* message?

He glanced at the hospital, wondering if his sister were responsible. Surely Audrey didn't work that fast, though. While he wouldn't put it past her, the message was from about an hour ago, long before he'd spilled everything to his sister.

He hit play and held the phone up to his ear.

"I know you need space or whatever," Dani said. Her voice was shaky and it shot him right through the heart. "But I need to talk to you." She sighed. "I got offered the promotion. The salary and benefits are good—in fact, it's everything I wanted and more. But when I saw they wanted me to sign a two-year contract, I told him I had to think about it. Shit, Wes, I don't know what to do."

She paused. "I thought that if we were together, even for a weekend, it'd make it impossible to get over you. But even without that, I can't seem to. I miss you. And I should've told you before, but…" He could hear her take a breath, then two. "I love you. I love you, and I'm sorry I screwed it all up."

The message ended, and all Wes could hear was his blood rushing in his ears. He'd heard that right, hadn't he? She loved him? And it didn't sound like it was in the totally platonic way. But she'd gotten the job offer. His work was here, his family was here—he was determined to help Audrey through physical therapy so it wouldn't be so hard on any one person.

Damn. Now he didn't know what to do. He rushed back into the hospital. Had to backtrack to the soda machine for a Diet Coke. If he wanted Audrey's attention, he'd need to bring her that drink. The elevator was taking forever so he ran up the stairs, the soda can so cold it was burning his hand.

He charged into her open door and tossed her the Diet Coke.

As she sipped it, he relayed the phone call, his nerves bouncing all over the place like he'd just downed all the caffeine. "What do I do? What do I say?"

"I'd go with a grand gesture. Maybe something impulsive and romantic. You've got at least one of those things down."

"Impulsive. Romantic." He swallowed past his dry throat. "I've got something that should cover both."

Chapter Nineteen

The numbers on the clock flipped closer and closer to her meeting with her boss, and Dani still didn't know what to do. She checked her e-mail again—nothing from Wes. Her phone was on, and he hadn't called.

Maybe he hasn't gotten my message yet.
Maybe I shouldn't have told him I love him.

Her stomach rolled and she wrapped her arms around her body. No, even if her confession didn't change Wes's mind, he deserved to know.

The digits at the bottom of her screen changed, advancing another number. Thirty-two minutes until Wayne expected a decision. Could she say no if Wes didn't want her anymore?

Could she say yes when she knew she'd still hate her job and forever wish she were in North Carolina instead?

Dani stood and rolled her neck one way and then the other. The stress was making her shoulders tight, and a pounding headache was edging its way in. Time to go outside, take some deep breaths, and figure out what she was going to do.

"Dani?" Linda came around the corner. "I'm supposed

to send you to the roof. Apparently we've got a new client, and Wayne wants you to be the one to meet him and bring him down to the office."

"From the roof?"

"Some bigwig. He's arriving by helicopter."

Of course. A helicopter. That wouldn't make her think of Wes *at all*. "Can't Bill do it? I was just about to take a quick break and grab a soda and some fresh air. Or maybe Mr. Bigwig can just drag his fancy butt down here himself?"

Two lines creased Linda's forehead. "You really want me to tell Wayne that?"

Dani blew out a long breath. "Of course not. I'll go up to the roof. Maybe I can at least catch a few gulps of fresh air."

Linda started to walk away, then abruptly spun back, took the pencil Dani was using to hold her bun in place out of her hair, and smiled. "Good luck."

Well, that was weird. Suddenly she was wondering if she got offered the job because she was female and Wayne thought she could reel in rich guys. So much for her improvement and skills.

She made her way to the elevator and punched the roof access button. Not that she wanted to play female escort, but she figured some lip gloss wouldn't kill her. She smoothed it on and popped a breath mint.

The evening air was perfect, warm but with a cool breeze. Dani inhaled and stepped out farther on the roof. Mr. Fancy Pants Client wasn't here yet, but she could see the helicopter nearing, the dark blue almost getting lost in the sky.

The helicopter was sleek and larger than the one Wes drove.

Wes. Thinking his name was a stab to the chest.

She glanced at her phone again, using it to check her e-mails. But of course there was nothing. Apparently it was time to suck it up and realize that she needed this job. As soon as she got back downstairs she'd sign the contract and take it to Wayne.

The wind from the helicopter stirred her hair, whipping it faster around her head the closer it came. The landing skids touched down and the loud whir of the rotor slowed. She thought she heard a door open, but she didn't see anyone.

Then a dark figure was coming around the front. The last rays of sunlight caught his hair, and she must have been losing it, because the guy had the same hair as Wes.

The same way of walking.

The same blue eyes.

Wes stopped in front of her, the air electric between them. She felt each thump of her heart, every breath that stole from her lips. She slowly reached out and gently poked his arm, thinking he might pop and the illusion would be gone.

Solid.

His lips kicked up on the right side, then the grin spread to the left, the way it always did.

She could feel his smile mirrored on her lips.

"I need to ask you a question," he said.

"I meant what I said," Dani blurted out, near tears with him here in front of her when she'd been so sure he'd given up on them. "I do love you. I love you so much I can hardly breathe, and I don't know how we'll work everything out, but I want to. I've never wanted anything more."

"Well, that's a relief because…" He pulled something out of his pocket and dropped onto one knee. A simple diamond on a silver band sat in the box, the still-spinning rotors causing light to wink off it at intervals. "Danielle Caridad Morales Vega, will you be engaged to me for real this time?"

She stared down at him, her mind trying to catch up to what he'd just asked. "You want to be engaged to me? Like the kind of engaged where we get married?"

"That's the basic idea, yeah."

The tears forming in her eyes started to spill over, no

chance at stopping them now that the impact of what he was asking her was sinking in. "And you're sure we wouldn't be jumping into it too fast?"

"I'm sure that I'd take you to Vegas tonight and marry you if you want. I'll wait a year and have the ceremony in the museum. Or a church wedding. Or a big to-do in a swanky hotel. I'm sure that I want to marry you and spend the rest of my life with you. I love you, Dani. So just say yes."

She felt that rush she always experienced before an adventure with Wes, but this was about a million times stronger. She dove onto him, throwing her arms around his neck and nearly toppling him over backward. Then his arms came around her and their mouths and bodies were pressed together. She parted her lips as he kissed her deeper, igniting heat and desire and a hundred other happy emotions that were buzzing through her like fireworks.

"Just so you know, I'm taking that as a yes," he mumbled against her lips.

"It's a yes." She put her hand on his face, running it across the stubble. "I want to go home to North Carolina with you. Where I belong."

The next thing she knew he was standing up, lifting her in his arms as he did so.

"I should probably go quit my job," she said.

He bounced her higher and strode toward the helicopter. "It can wait. I want to show you the roomy backseat in my helicopter."

"But whatever will we do with all that room?"

A mischievous grin that sent her body tingling with anticipation curved his lips. "Five bucks I can figure something out."

Epilogue

Dani glanced around the room, at the whir of all the last minute getting-ready-type things like more hairspray and perfume, her soon to be sisters-in-law and Brynn in their royal blue bridesmaid dresses. There were so many times she and Wes talked about scrapping the wedding planning and going to Vegas, but after she'd seen the atrium of the Levine Museum decked out in dark blue and silver with flowers and lights, throughout, she was glad they'd waited to get married in a place that meant something to both of them. Their nerdy love of history had brought them together in the first place, and the venue seemed like a good way to honor a friendship that'd turned to more.

Closing her eyes, she replayed Wes dropping on one knee and asking her to be engaged to him for real. Falling for him had been a wonderful, unexpected adventure, and she'd forever be glad for their fake engagement scheme that had led them to this moment. Then, after she'd said yes with her lips more than words, he'd carried her to the helicopter, deposited her in the backseat, and kissed her like he meant to make up for all the years they should've been kissing.

They'd had sex in many unchartered places since their first time in the back of the helicopter, from woods to a boat on a mountain lake to a secluded waterfall, but that first time, releasing all that pent up romantic tension would be one she never forgot. That night she'd wanted to slowly take in every detail, yet go fast because she could hardly wait to discover the one part of Wes she hadn't yet.

She felt that way right now, too—wanted to enjoy the buzz and the lights and the trip down the aisle, yet wanted it to be over so she and Wes would be married already and off on their honeymoon.

Finally it was time to line up, so they left the room and headed to the back of the aisle. Mama stepped up next to Dani—she was giving her away in the absence of Papa. Abuela Morales was up near the front, her oxygen tank left in the car since she refused to have pictures with her "damned oxygen tube" covering her face. Her health was good, though she tired out quickly and breathed better with the oxygen. Luckily, with the adventure tour business already turning a profit, Dani and Wes were able to help out with the medical bills. The fact that Wes never hesitated to help, and talked to Mama and Abuela over the phone almost as much as she did made her love him even more.

The wedding party headed down the aisle, two by two, the way they'd practiced the day before. Then the "Wedding March" started and everyone stood. Dani cracked her knuckles—something Wes always winced at—and then started down the aisle, wishing for a basketball to hold instead of a useless bouquet of flowers.

But then Wes's face came into view and her nerves slowly melted away. A slow smile curved his lips, the corners of his eyes crinkling, and excitement tingled through her veins as love filled her from the inside out. His hair was long enough to curl around his ears, his face sporting a five o clock shadow. Dani knew his mom and sisters had asked him a hundred times about getting a trim and making sure his face was shaved, but Dani preferred him slightly scruffy, and since she was the bride, she got what she wanted.

Wes leaned in and kissed Mama on the cheek, whispered something to her that made her smile, and then reached for Dani's hand. He slipped his fingers between hers and curled them around her palm. She glanced at him, feeling the grin stretching her lips. A sense of camaraderie passed between them, like they were almost to pull off the biggest stunt yet.

• • •

Wes held tightly to Dani's hand, happiness bubbling up in him. His friend Connor had kept asking him if he was nervous leading up today, but this moment was all he'd wanted since they'd first gotten engaged—the second time. The real time. Honestly, though, he'd always wanted Dani in his life forever. He just didn't know he'd be lucky enough for it to be as his wife.

His mom and sisters had done a wonderful job getting the atrium transformed to the fanciest place he'd ever been and it was good to have all his friends next to him—he had a feeling they were all about to become married men soon, and every one of them was way more thrilled than they might admit. If this was the reward for admitting it, though, he'd shout it from the rooftops.

As he and Dani approached the front, he took a moment to look her from head to toe. When she'd come down the aisle, she was so pretty he could hardly breathe. Now he could see the way the dress scooped low in the back, displaying her bronze, toned skin. He couldn't help but reach out and run his fingers across the opening. "You found another backwards dress," he whispered.

One corner of her lips turned up as her gaze met his.

"Just a little more forward," the preacher said, urging them closer to him.

Wes ran his fingers over Dani's soft skin one more time—the way he planned to all night, every chance he could, and definitely when they were dancing, her body pressed against his. He took her hand again and they made the last few steps before turning to face each other. She swept her bangs behind her ear and they immediately fell forward in that way he loved. Then he stared into her dark brown eyes as the preacher started the ceremony.

And Wes knew that he and Dani were about to embark on their greatest adventure yet.

Keep reading for an exclusive sneak peek at Cindi's upcoming book, *Just One of the Groomsmen*!

Chapter One

The boat house came into view and Addie's excitement level went from its already high seven to a solid ten. An emergency meeting had been called, and all of the guys were going to be in attendance. Every single one, including the guy she'd been dying to see for so long that she'd almost worried their sporadic phone calls, texts, and messages were the only way they'd ever communicate again.

Addie pulled up next to the sleek, compact car she'd have to make fun of later—right now it meant that Tucker Crawford was here in the flesh, and within a few minutes, the whole gang would be here as well. She wasn't sure why Shep had called the meeting, but it took her back to high school when so many of their evenings and weekends were spent here at the Crawfords' boathouse. Lazy afternoons and countless poker games. Nights spent celebrating team wins or commiserating over losses, whether it was the high school team that the guys had all played for, Crimson Tide football, or our NFL teams, on which they were a house divided—it'd led to some of Tucker and her most heated exchanges.

The scent of Cypress, swampy lake water, and moss hit her as she climbed out of the beater truck she often drove, and since she was hoping for a minute or two with Tucker before everyone else showed up, she rushed up the pathway, her rapid steps echoing against the wood once she hit the plank leading to the boat. "Tucker?"

"Addie?"

She heard his voice but didn't see him. Then she rounded the front of the boat, where the chairs and grill were set up, and there he was. Even taller and wider than she remembered, his copper brown hair styled shorter than he wore it in high school, although the wave in it meant there were always a couple of strands that did their own thing, no matter how much gel he put in it.

A laugh escaped as she took a few long strides and launched herself at him, her arms going around his neck. "I'll be damned, you actually made it this time."

Using the arm he'd wrapped around her lower back he lifted her off her feet and squeezed tight enough to send her breath out over his shoulder. "I'm sorry for accidentally standing you up a few times. It's stupid how hard it's been to get away this past year."

"That's what happens when you decide to go and be some big city lawyer." She pulled back to get another look at one of her best and very oldest friends. She had so much to tell him that she didn't know where to start. Thanks to his crazy work schedule, even their phone calls and texts had slowed to a trickle. Despite working at the law firm for nearly two years, he was still one of the junior attorneys, which meant he ended up doing all the time-consuming research for the partners. Before that he'd been busy with law school, and while she wasn't usually the mushy hugger-type, she didn't want to completely let go, just in case she had to go another year without seeing him.

Only now that she was focusing on every single detail, from the familiar blue eyes to his strong, freshly-shaven jawline, to—holy crap, when did he get jacked shoulders and pecs and arms like that? Was lifting bulky legal files muscle-building. If so, maybe she needed to recommend it as part of her clients' physical therapy regimens.

His gaze ran over her as well, most likely assessing the ways she'd changed—or more likely hadn't—but for a quick second, her body got the wrong message, a swirl going through her stomach and her pulse quickening.

And before she thought better of it, she reached up and ran her hand through his hair, loosening the hold the gel had on it. He could definitely pull off the clean-cut lawyer look, but she preferred the more-relaxed version. Maybe that version would also help her keep from looking at him as something other than…well, him. Tucker Crawford. The boy who'd once landed her in detention because he'd dared her to put super glue on the teacher's whiteboard makers while he distracted him with a question; boy who'd challenged her to a deviled egg eating competition at the town festival—to this day the sight or scent of a deviled egg made her stomach roll.

Tucker's hand went to her hip, a shallow breath fell from her lips, and time froze…

"Crawford? Where you at?" Shep's booming voice broke whatever weirdo vibes were trickling into the reunion she'd been awaiting for what seemed like forever, and she dropped her hand, just in time for Shep, Easton, and Ford to come around the corner to the deck of the boat.

"Murph!" They yelled when they saw her, and then they exchanged some high fives and a few bro-hugs on their way to give Tucker the same treatment. She saw the rest of the guys around town now and then, but it was harder to get together now that everyone had careers and other obligations, and they hadn't hung out in way too long. Funny how in high school they couldn't wait to get older so they could do whatever they wanted, and instead they ended up having less free time than ever.

Shep placed two six packs of beer on the desk railing. "Before we get this party started, I guess I should let you all know what we're celebrating." The hint of worry she'd felt since getting the urgent meeting text evaporated. The message had been so vague—typical guy, although her mom and sister had often accused her of the same thing.

Addie sat on the edge of the table, and when Tucker bumped her over with his hip, she scooted. Then the table wobbled, and Tucker's hand shot out and wrapped around her upper arm as she worked to rebalance herself.

He chuckled. "Guess we're heavier than we used to be."

"Speak for yourself," she said, shoving his arm, glad things were back to normal. With a hint of noticing the firm press of his shoulder and thigh and the warmth radiating off his body.

"So, you guys might recall I've been seeing Sexy Lexi, going on a year now."

"How could we forget?" Addie quipped. "You talk about her non-stop." She glanced at Tucker. "Seriously, we go to get a beer and it's just Lexi this, and Lexi that."

Shep didn't scowl at her like she'd expected, grinning that twitterpated grin he now wore instead.

"She's actually very lovely." Addie curled her hands around the table. While his southern belle girlfriend worked to hold it at bay, she didn't think Lexi was her biggest fan, and she hated always having to calm down her friendship with the guys in order to not upset the balance of their relationships. Hopefully a little more time and getting to know each other, and Lexi would understand that Will Shepherd was more like a brother than anything.

All of the guys were.

Tucker's hand covered hers and he gave it a reassuring squeeze.

Okay, maybe she was questioning the past tense of that *were* the tiniest bit.

Crap, she didn't know. But she could say for sure that she and Shep were more sibling-like than the rest. It wasn't the first time her friends' girlfriends were wary of her, and she doubted it'd be the last. Sometimes she worried she'd get left behind, just because she was a girl in a group of guys. That was a technicality, though. It wasn't that she didn't have female friends or that she didn't know a lot of great women; it was that she'd grown up with these guys and forged memories and they liked to do the same things she did.

It was why she'd gone by "Murph" more often than Addison Murphy, or any other variation thereof. Thanks to her love of comfy, sporty clothes, she'd been voted "most likely to start her own sweatshirt line" in high school, a title she was proud to have, by the way.

Easton had been voted "most likely to end up in jail," and ironically enough he was now a cop, something they all teased him about. Which reminded her...

"Don't let me forget to make fun of your prissy car when this meeting is over with," Addie whispered to Tucker.

He opened his mouth, assumedly to defend himself and then Shep cleared his throat.

"*Anyway*, last weekend I asked Lexi to marry me." A huge grin spread across his face. "And she said yes."

They offered their congratulations, and after a few claps on the back and obligatory jokes about ball and chains, Shep said, "I want you guys to be in my wedding. To be my groomsmen."

Addie's stomach dropped. "You guys" usually included her, but she knew the word "groomsmen" didn't. "Ha! You guys are all gonna have to wear stuffy penguin suits and take hundreds of pictures. Have fun with that."

Shep looked at her, and a sense of foreboding prickled her skin. "Before you go celebrating too much, you're in the wedding party, too. I told Lexi that I wanted you as one of my groomsmen."

While his girlfriend—make that fiancée—was pretty patient and understanding of Shep's crazy, out-there ideas, she was also *extremely* girly. Like she wore dress and heels more often than not—including to the local bar, which wasn't a dress-and-heels kind of joint—and belonged to one of those societies that threw things like tea parties and galas. "I'm sure that went over about as well as coming out as a vegan in the middle of Sunday dinner."

"She understands that you're just one of the guys," Shep said, and a hint of hope rose up. She hated that lately she felt left out. Add to that the spinning-wheels sensation and her life needed a shakeup.

Maybe I should've taken that job. It would've meant moving over three hours away from Mom, Dad, and Nonna Hutchins, but she still wondered if she'd missed an opportunity. She'd witnessed the sorrow of her sister moving a state away. They'd been so upset, asking if they'd done something wrong, because how couldn't you want to stay in Uncertainty, Alabama, where everyone knew everyone, and they all thought that entitled them to being all up in your business?

"But she's also more traditional, her family even more so."

"I understand," Addie said. "I don't think I'd look very good in a tux anyway, and my own mother would probably die twice over it."

"Which is why..." Shep straightened, his hazel eyes on me. "Lexi and I came up with a compromise. You'll be a groomsmen in name, and when it comes to all the usual pre-wedding stuff, but in order to be part of the wedding party you're going to have to wear the same dress and shoes as the bridesmaids." The rest of the words came out in a fast blur, like he hoped if he talked fast enough I might miss them. "And you might have to dress up one or two other times, like at the rehearsal dinner and maybe even the bridal shower."

The guys burst out laughing. "Murph in a dress and heels," Easton said. "That'll be the day."

Addie picked up the nearest object she could find—a coaster—and chucked it at his head. It bounced off but didn't deter him from laughing.

The table shook, and when she looked at Tucker, he had a fist over his mouth to try to smother his laughter.

"You too?"

"Please, Addie," Shep said. "I know it's not your thing, but I can't imagine you not being part of this." He shot a challenging glare at the group of them. "And spare me the jokes about actually caring about my wedding. I never thought I'd be this happy, but I am, and I want you guys there. I need you guys with me on this."

This time, the "you guys" definitely included her. Which made it that much easier to say, "I'm in. I'll do whatever you need me to."

• • •

Man it was good to be back in town, even if only for a quick weekend. Tucker had been working hours and hours on end, thinking that after putting in two years at the law firm he'd have enough experience and clout to slow down a little. It never slowed down, though, his work load multiplying at an impossible-to-keep-up-with pace. He'd had to cancel his last two trips home with lame, last-minute texts and calls, but now that he was seated around the poker table with his friends, all felt right with the world.

"You're bluffing," Addie said when Easton threw several chips into the pot. She matched his bet and then they laid down their cards, her full house easily beating his pair of Aces. "Read 'em and weep, sucker." She leaned over the table to gather her winnings, and Tucker's gaze ran down the line of her body. Okay, so maybe one thing felt a little off, but it didn't exactly feel not-right, even if he knew he should shut down all thoughts of Addie's body and how amazing she looked.

He cracked a smile at the thought of her in a dress and heels, bouquet in hand. It wasn't that they'd never seen her wear a dress; it was that she loathed them, and she'd once slugged him in the shoulder for even mentioning her dress-wearing at her sister's wedding. The skirt had been long and baggy, and the real tragedy was that she couldn't toss around the pigskin—her mom said it'd ruin her nice clothes, and then added that it was an "inappropriate wedding activity, anyway." So then they'd *both* had to sit there with their hands folded in their laps and it was boring as hell, an emotion he'd rarely experienced around her.

"Your poker face is crap, Crawford. I know you're thinking about how funny it is that I just agreed to wear a freaking bridesmaid's dress, and if you don't want me to jam that beer you're drinking where the sun don't shine, I suggest you wipe the smirk off your face." She pointed her finger around the table. "That goes for all of you."

"I appreciate you going along with it," Shep said. "I told Lexi that you'd probably punch me or kick me in the balls just for suggesting it."

"Lucky for you, you were too far away and wearing that love-struck grin that makes me take pity on you."

"When someone basically says thank you, maybe don't follow that up by insulting them." Shep began dealing the cards he'd just finished shuffling. "Just a suggestion."

"This is why so many guys in town are scared of you," Easton said with a laugh.

She clucked her tongue. "They are not."

All of the guys nodded, and Tucker found himself nodding even though he hadn't lived in town for the better part of a decade. It'd been like that since high school, and the selfish part of him was glad that no guy had come in and swept her off her feet. Not that Addie would ever let some guy do the sweeping. Still, with her blond hair that was forever in a high ponytail and the smattering of freckles across her nose that drew you right to them and her big brown eyes, it was surprising she'd stayed mostly single. Or maybe she hadn't told him about her boyfriends, the way he'd never really discussed his girlfriends with her. There weren't many to talk about since he'd been so busy, but he also didn't want anything to get in the way of getting back to them when they managed to find time to talk.

Ford pinned her with a look. "Addie, when guys come in for physical therapy, you tell them to stop crying over something your grandma could do."

"Well, she could! My nonna is tougher than most of the dudes who come in whining about their injuries. Then they don't want to put in the work it takes to get over them. Telling them my grandma could do the things I'm instructing them to do is motivating."

"Not to ask you out," Ford said, and snickers went around the table.

"Very funny. Being scared of me and being undateable are two different things."

"You're hardly undateable," Tucker said, the words similar to exchanges they'd had in high school.

"Yeah, but it's nearly impossible to find someone who doesn't already know too much about me—or me about them—and even if I manage that, then I introduce him to you guys, and things unravel pretty quickly after that."

"Maybe with one of us getting hitched, we'll be less intimidating." Shep tossed in the ante and everyone else did the same.

"I'm sure it's me," Addie muttered. "Now, do you guys want to talk about my pathetic dating life, or do you want me to take all your money?"

"Wow, what great options," Tucker deadpanned. "Not sure why anyone would be scared of you. Couldn't be all the threats."

She turned those big eyes on him and cocked an eyebrow. "Listen, city boy. Maybe you can just flash your shiny car and some Benjamins to get your way where you live, but here we still live and die by the same code."

He leaned in, challenge firing in his veins. "And that is...?"

"Loser buys beer."

Shep revealed the flop and Tucker watched everyone's faces for signs of what cards they had or were hoping for. They did a few more rounds of betting as more cards were revealed, and at the end it came down to him and Addie.

She called his bet and then proceeded to take the last of his chips.

They played until Addie had pretty much cleaned everyone out, then one by one they left, save the two of them.

"Are you staying at the boathouse tonight?" she asked as she gathered her keys off the table outside.

He wasn't sure if she was offering him a place to crash or just curious. His parents had relocated shortly after he started law school, and he'd hated how uprooted he'd felt even though he didn't technically live in Uncertainty anymore. He'd asked them to hold off on selling the boathouse, and when Dad claimed he couldn't, Tucker bought it himself. Having to visit them in a different city made it that much harder to get back here, and he'd already seen repairs that would need to be made. "I like it out here on the lake, so I would prefer it even if my parents' hadn't sold their place."

A smile curved her lips as she ran her hand over the deck railing. "I love this mini-house and all of our memories here."

"Me, too." He folded his forearms on the railing and looked over at her, watching the breeze stir the strands of hair. "Tonight was the most fun I've had in a long time."

Her grin widened, and it lit up her whole face. The moon glowed off her features—pretty features he couldn't help gazing at. Growing up with her had left him so used to how she looked that he'd forgotten how beautiful she was, and he didn't really notice until he'd gone somewhere else and realized how unique she and the relationships they had was. No one else was like her. It was why she was one of his very best friends, and that meant stifling the urge to ask her to stay the night with him. He wanted to think it could be just like old times when they'd crash out on the couch or tiny bed.

Except now he might be tempted to curl her to him, and not just for warmth or minor cuddling. It must just be that he hadn't had time off in forever, the fun he'd admitted to leaving him more buzzed than the beer. Or that he hadn't been out with a woman in so long that his thoughts were running wild. Either way, he needed to leash them before they ruined one of the purest, best relationships he had in his life.

"Good night, Tucker." She turned to go, but then abruptly spun around and hugged him tight. "I understand that your job is demanding, but don't be a stranger."

He squeezed her back, taking a whiff of her shampoo—something fruity that smelled good and made him want to bury his nose in the silky strands, another sign that he was drunk and nostalgic, and he should definitely let her go now.

"At least with Shep getting married you've got another

excuse to come down and spend more than a weekend here," she said.

He nodded. "Yeah, it's good to have an excuse." What he wanted was an excuse not to go back to his cold, generic apartment and mind-numbing job.

What he wanted was to return to his friends and the town he loved, and he wasn't sure how he could possibly go back and be satisfied with his old life after tonight showed him everything that was missing from it.

Acknowledgments

Thanks to my awesome editor, Stacy Abrams, for asking if I wanted to write a Bliss book, suggesting awesome additions, and always making my books better. Thanks to Alycia Tornetta for a tweet that got my mind whirring and had me plotting out this book instead of sleeping, as well as all of your insight and hard work. Thanks to Rachel Harris for always being there, your boundless enthusiasm, and helping me decide that Wes should be a helicopter pilot. Everything fell into place after that. And thanks to my sister, Randa, who suggested I "severely maim" instead of kill off a character. I'm glad I listened and went for more severely injured. That conversation still cracks me up, though.

Thanks to the entire support team at Entangled. All the authors and editors and my publicists, Heather Riccio and Elana Johnson. I'm so lucky to be part of the Entangled family! Thanks to Liz Pelletier for always being so open and willing to share. In addition to that Vegas trip being fun, the information I learned there also helped me write the ending of this book. Maybe what happens in Vegas doesn't always stay there. (Don't worry, most of it does.)

Thanks to Dr. Tom Hanchett from the Levine Museum of the New South, who was so nice and talked to me about the Good Samaritan Hospital's chapel so I could get it as accurate as possible, since I couldn't fly there and check it out like I wanted to (maybe someday). Thanks to my uncle, Scott Harmsen, for answering my questions about helicopters. To all my family for putting up with me when I go into crazy-writer mode. To all my Twitter friends, you guys make me laugh and keep me going and you just rock! Special shout-out to #TeamKilt, #TheTimeZonesWillNotDefeatUsBookClub, and Andrea Thompson, who makes me laugh, provides encouragement, and burns food along with me. And where would I be without Anne Eliot, the best cheerleader/writing buddy I could ask for? So amazing watching dreams come true with you.

And thanks to my husband, Michael, for his endless support and love. Another example that dreams come true. And to anyone who's read my books, thank you!

About the Author

Cindi Madsen is a *USA Today* bestselling author of contemporary romance and young adult novels. She sits at her computer every chance she gets, plotting, revising, and falling in love with her characters. Sometimes it makes her a crazy person. Without it, she'd be even crazier. She has way too many shoes, but can always find a reason to buy a pretty new pair, especially if they're sparkly, colorful, or super tall. She loves music and dancing and wishes summer lasted all year long. She lives in Colorado (where summer is most definitely NOT all year long) with her husband, three children, an overly-dramatic tomcat, & an adorable one-eyed kitty named Agent Fury.

You can visit Cindi at: www.cindimadsen.com, where you can sign up for her newsletter to get all the up-to-date information on her books.

Follow her on Twitter @cindimadsen.

Discover the **Accidentally in Love** *series…*

ACT LIKE YOU LOVE ME

AN OFFICER AND A REBEL

RESISTING THE HERO

Also by Cindi Madsen

SECOND CHANCE RANCH

CRAZY FOR THE COMPETITION

THE BAD BOY'S BABY

UNTIL YOU'RE MINE

UNTIL WE'RE MORE

GETTING LUCKY NUMBER SEVEN

ANATOMY OF A PLAYER

CRAZY PUCKING LOVE

CONFESSIONS OF A FORMER PUCK BUNNY

NAILED IT

12 STEPS TO MR. RIGHT

JUST ONE OF THE GROOMSMEN

CINDERELLA SCREWED ME OVER

JUST JILTED

OPERATION PROM DATE

ALL THE BROKEN PIECES

Find your Bliss with these great releases...

Romancing His Rival
an *Accidentally Yours* novel by Jennifer Shirk

Elena Mason doesn't often hate people, but she *hates* her ex-fiancé's insufferable best man, Lucas Albright III. She just knows Lucas is the one who talked her ex out of getting married—so Lucas is clearly the cause of all her problems. And now she's expected to *work* with him? Oh, heck no. But it turns out he had a great reason to end her engagement... So what happens when fighting starts feeling a whole lot like falling in love?

The Firefighter's Pretend Fiancée
a *Shadow Creek* novel by Victoria James

Leaving Shadow Creek was the hardest thing Molly Mayberry's ever had to do. A chance of a lifetime position at the local hospital means going home and facing her past, including the fiancé she ran out on. Ben Matthews is still the sexy, sweet man she left behind...and apparently still her fiancé.

IN THE DOG HOUSE
an *Appletree Cove* novel by Traci Hall

Ten years ago, Jackson Hardy joined the Marines, leaving behind a woman he still dreams about. When he's called home to care for his ten-year-old nephew, no one is more shocked than he to run into Emma again. Or to still have those same feelings. But Jackson isn't looking for love, and neither is Emma, especially not with him. His precocious nephew, though, and a retriever named Bandit, are about to change that.

THE SHERIFF'S LITTLE MATCHMAKER
a *Rose Creek, Texas* novel by Carrie Nichols

When teacher Sasha Honeycutt kisses a handsome cowboy in a bar on a dare, she never expects to see him again. To her surprise, though, he walks through the door of her classroom for a parent-teacher conference. Sheriff Remy Fontenot might be sexy as sin, but Sasha has no interest in falling for another policeman. Rose Creek is her fresh start after being "that poor widow." Only, Remy's precocious daughter has big plans for them…